Katie stepped into the back of the Rolls-Royce...and came face-to-face with Adam Braddock

What was he doing here? And what would she say when he demanded to know why a waitress was climbing into his Rolls-Royce?

"Ms. Canton? I'm Adam Braddock," he said, extending his hand over his laptop computer.

"Hello," she said, realizing he hadn't recognized her. Yet.

A phone rang—conveniently positioned in a door console—and Adam picked it up. Katie could feel the energy in his conversation. There was frustration beneath his incredibly perfect surface. She'd thought him attractive in the restaurant, but here in his natural habitat, he was quite extraordinarily handsome. Katie leaned back against the supple leather seat and watched him in profile. What would it be like, she wondered, to have Adam Braddock focus that same intensity on her?

When he realized she was the waitress he'd met at the Torrid Tomato restaurant, and not the fancy events coordinator she just might fi

D1462965

Dear Reader,

Harlequin American Romance has rounded up the best romantic reading to help you celebrate Valentine's Day. Start off with the final installment in the MAITLAND MATERNITY: TRIPLETS, QUADS & QUINTS series. *The McCallum Quintuplets* is a special three-in-one volume featuring *New York Times* bestselling author Kasey Michaels, Mindy Neff and Mary Anne Wilson.

BILLION-DOLLAR BRADDOCKS, Karen Toller Whittenburg's new family-connected miniseries, premiers this month with *The C.E.O.'s Unplanned Proposal*. In this Cinderella story, a small-town waitress is swept into the Braddock world of wealth and power and puts eldest brother Adam Braddock's bachelor status to the test. Next, in Bonnie Gardner's *Sgt. Billy's Bride*, an air force controller is in desperate need of a fiancée to appease his beloved, ailing mother, so he asks a beautiful stranger to become his wife. Can love bloom and turn their pretend engagement into wedded bliss? Finally, we welcome another new author to the Harlequin American family. Sharon Swan makes her irresistible debut with *Cowboys and Cradles*.

Enjoy this month's offerings, and be sure to return next month when Harlequin American Romance launches a new cross-line continuity, THE CARRADIGNES: AMERICAN ROYALTY, with *The Improperly Pregnant Princess* by Jacqueline Diamond.

Wishing you happy reading,

Melissa Jeglinski
Associate Senior Editor
Harlequin American Romance

THE C.E.O.'S
UNPLANNED PROPOSAL
Karen Toller Whittenburg

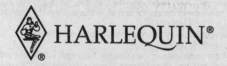

TORONTO • NEW YORK • LONDON
AMSTERDAM • PARIS • SYDNEY • HAMBURG
STOCKHOLM • ATHENS • TOKYO • MILAN • MADRID
PRAGUE • WARSAW • BUDAPEST • AUCKLAND

To Paula and Genell, my companions on the journey.
And to Cathy Gillen Thacker, for encouragement above
and beyond. Thanks, Cathy!

ISBN 0-373-16910-8

THE C.E.O.'S UNPLANNED PROPOSAL

Copyright © 2002 by Karen Whittenburg Crane.

Visit us at www.eHarlequin.com

Printed in U.S.A.

ABOUT THE AUTHOR

Karen Toller Whittenburg is a native Oklahoman who fell in love with books the moment she learned to read and has been addicted to the written word ever since. She wrote stories as a child, but it wasn't until she discovered romance fiction that she felt compelled to write, fascinated by the chance to explore the positive power of love in people's lives. She grew up in Sand Springs (an historic town on the Arkansas River), attended Oklahoma State University and now lives in Tulsa with her husband, a professional photographer.

Books by Karen Toller Whittenburg

HARLEQUIN AMERICAN ROMANCE

Don't miss any of our special offers. Write to us at the following address for information on our newest releases.

Harlequin Reader Service
U.S.: 3010 Walden Ave., P.O. Box 1325, Buffalo, NY 14269
Canadian: P.O. Box 609, Fort Erie, Ont. L2A 5X3

BRADDOCK FAMILY TREE

Archer Braddock m. Jane (d)

James Braddock

m.
Lily Hamilton (d)

Adam Braddock ①

m.
Mariah Dellin (*)

Bryce Braddock ②

m.
Catherine Latiker (d)

Peter Braddock ③

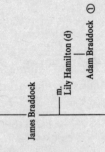

(d) deceased
* divorced
① *The C.E.O.'s Unplanned Proposal 2/02*
② *The Playboy's Office Romance 3/02*
③ *The Blacksheep's Arranged Marriage 4/02*

Prologue

Archer Braddock beat the rain to the top of the steps of Number 37 Lancashire and raised his cane to rap smartly on the front door. He liked the sound of wood on wood, found the cheerful chiming of a doorbell both annoying and intrusive, but a knock…ah, a knock was resonant discourse, an "I-have-business-within" announcement. Hadn't he always told Janey he could tell as much about a man by his knock on the door as by his handshake? If she were here now, she'd remind him that using a cane instead of his knuckles was cheating somewhat on that theory, but arthritis had long since taken the strength from his hands, and death had stolen away his Janey. Still, she was the reason he was outside this particular door on this particular day, waiting to be admitted. "Ah, Janey, Janey," he murmured softly. "Happy Anniversary, my dear."

The door swung open just as the cold, January rain started in earnest and without waiting for a formal invitation, he stepped into the sheltered entryway. "Archer Braddock," he announced himself to the crisp, somber-faced butler. "I have a two o'clock appointment with Mrs. Fairchild."

"Yes, sir. We've been expecting you." The butler closed the door and Archer doffed his hat, sending a fine splatter of raindrops across the marbled tile. "Did you have an umbrella, sir?" the man asked as he expertly assisted in the removal of Archer's top-coat and gloves.

"No. No, I'm afraid not." There was one in the car, of course. His own man, Abbott, would never have let him leave the house without being properly equipped for every conceivable shift in the weather—it was a matter of pride among butlers, it seemed—but Archer had forgotten the umbrella when he'd dismissed the car. He hadn't wanted any-one, including his completely trustworthy driver, to know where his appointment was today or with whom.

"Your scarf, sir?" The butler stood ready to ac-cept the gray cashmere muffler, and Archer allowed his hand to linger a moment in the soft folds before he pulled it from around his neck. It was a gift from Janey one long-ago winter and a present reminder that she was never far from his side…if only in warm memory. And today, more than ever, Archer needed to feel her near.

The butler carefully folded the scarf and set it be-side Archer's hat on a marble top credenza. "Mrs. Fairchild is in the study," he said. "If you'll follow me, please."

Archer settled his balance over the cane and set off after the butler. Not so many years ago, he'd largely have ignored his surroundings, taken for granted the beauty of luxury, and already been focused on the meeting ahead. But seventy-eight summers had taught him life was in a big enough rush without him adding to it and so he walked slower now, by choice as much as necessity. He'd never been to Ilsa's home before, never had occasion or reason to be there until now and he was—as silly as it seemed—a little nervous. But the quiet charm of her home put some of his more niggling doubts to rest. Touches of elegance such as an Aubusson rug in the foyer, a Picasso on the wall leading upstairs, vases of fresh-cut flowers on mahogany tables in the open foyer were interspersed with simple indications—an old woven basket holding garden shears and a pair of women's flowery cotton gloves, a pair of half-glasses sitting atop an upended book—that the woman who lived in this house was not overly concerned with appearances.

The butler led the way across the foyer to an open doorway and announced crisply, "Mr. Archer Braddock."

"Mr. Braddock." Ilsa Fairchild rose from an upholstered wing chair before a cozy fire to greet him warmly. "Right on time. Please come in."

Archer stepped over the threshold, calling himself three kinds of a fool for setting out on this errand, for being an old man who still wished to believe in fairy tales and magic, but he extended his hand to her with a deceptively confident smile. "Thank you for seeing me on such short notice," he said. "I don't often make the trip into Providence."

"I'm thrilled that you called. It's wonderful to see you again." She accepted his handshake and then indicated with a gesture that he should be seated in the matching wing chair across from hers. "It's been...what? Five years since we worked together on the library fund-raiser?"

"About that," Archer agreed. "There have been so many of them through the years, I've lost track of which was which. The library always was one of Janey's pet projects, you know."

"Mine, as well." Ilsa resumed her seat, graciously allowing him time to settle his less-than-graceful body into the chair while she addressed the butler. "Robert? Would you please bring us some tea and—" she looked a question at Archer "—coffee?"

He sank onto the cushions, grateful to be sitting after his walk in the moist afternoon air. "I would appreciate a cup of coffee," he agreed.

Robert nodded acquiescence and withdrew, closing the double doors and enclosing Archer in the welcome warmth of the room and Ilsa's smile. She still looked like a youngster to him although he knew she was in her early fifties, at most only a year or two younger than his own son, James. Age and experience had mined her beauty, faceted her charm, replacing lustrous youth with polished grace. She was still beautiful, tall, elegantly slender, with hair that had once been the color of new copper, but had faded to a muted auburn. Her gray eyes held the light of laughter and the knowledge of sorrow, but mostly the deep-set twinkle of a true believer and that, above all else, was the reason he had come.

"I was in Amsterdam when I heard about Mrs. Braddock's passing." Ilsa leaned slightly toward him with sympathy and the understanding of a widow for a widower. "I'm so sorry I couldn't have attended the funeral."

It would be two years in March since that day and still the word bothered him as much now as then. "Celebration," he corrected gently. "Funeral has such a final sound to it and, well, the truth is, I prefer to remember that day as a celebration of her life. She would have wanted to go out on a high note, you know."

"I wish I'd known her better," Ilsa said. "But any woman who was so obviously adored by the men in her life had to have been very special, indeed."

"She was the love of my life, and I knew it the first second I laid eyes on her." Archer leaned against the firmly cushioned chair back, shifting the crook of the sturdy, cherrywood cane—yet another lasting gift from his Janey—to the chair's curved arm. "I know the value of love and the benefits of a good marriage. That's why I'm here. My dear Mrs. Fairchild…may I call you Ilsa? I find myself in need of a…matchmaker."

ILSA WAS SELDOM surprised by comments made inside the privacy of her study. Her clients tended to be nervous, unsure and somewhat embarrassed about their decision to seek her services. Often, the person seated across from her had no real idea of what she could and couldn't do for them, nor was there any clear understanding of what, exactly, a matchmaker's role was in the twenty-first century. With experience, Ilsa had learned to be forthright in setting a businesslike tone for these initial meetings, in establishing her credentials and outlining her strategies. It prevented problems down the road, but usually the client needed to first feel at ease and the business aspect didn't come into play until after Robert had served tea, and the social niceties were duly dispatched.

Archer Braddock was obviously not her typical client.

"You need a matchmaker?" she repeated, knowing her surprise echoed in the words. "For yourself?"

A hoarse rumble of amusement edged past his immediate smile and became a deep, satisfied chuckle. "Ah, Ilsa, it was worth the trip up from Sea Change just for that." He lifted a wizened hand to his mouth, as if to cover his laughter, but when he let it drop back onto the arm of the chair, his amusement was still very much in evidence. "Thank you, my dear, for believing even for an instant that I could still fancy myself going a courting. But the truth is, I'll be seventy-nine at the end of June and it's too late in my life to go looking for love, even if Janey wasn't—as my grandsons would say—such a tough act to follow."

Ilsa could feel a blush warming her cheeks and had to wonder what it was about the Braddock men that made her feel like such an ingenue. James had had the same effect on her when they were in school together, and the few times she had encountered him since. And now within the first ten minutes, she had reverted to speaking first and thinking afterward with his father, too. Of course, it could have had something to do with the fact that the Braddock name was synonymous with wealth and power, not only in Rhode Island, but up and down the Eastern seaboard.

Maybe even in the whole western hemisphere! But Ilsa was no stranger to the privilege of family name and fortune herself and suspected her reaction was rooted in a much more basic reality. James and Archer Braddock were old world gentlemen, possessed of an elemental charm, a warm, earthy attraction and a sincere, somewhat awed regard for women. Archer had spent half a century deeply in love with his wife, while James—the last Ilsa had heard—was still seeking his perfect match. Still, there was some indefinable quality in both men that women responded to, naturally and without hesitation. Ilsa recognized it, even if she couldn't quite put a name to it.

Robert's tap on the door and subsequent entry with the tea tray was a more welcome interruption than she wanted to admit. Occupying her hands with the china cups and making sure the coffee was just the way her guest preferred it gave her time to regain a professional mien. No matter how influential, famous and powerful the Braddock family undeniably was, Archer Braddock had come to her as a client, and she would treat him as such. Which meant, despite an almost overwhelming impulse to ask about James—where he was, what he was doing, if he were married or not—she would keep her thoughts to herself and listen. If she'd learned anything about the people who sought out her services, she knew that listening was the key to it all. It was her gift, the listening. That and the ability to detect a spark of attraction where none was supposed to exist.

She'd barely swallowed her first sip of steaming Earl Grey, however, when Archer nailed her with the unexpected yet again. "You remember James?" he asked, as if there were some possibility she could have forgotten him. ''I believe the two of you were in school together at one time.''

Ilsa set her cup in its china saucer with a *ca-clink.* ''Yes, he was two years ahead of me at Exeter. He was also at Harvard with my husband, Ian. I haven't seen James in several years. How is he?''

''Engaged,'' Archer said with a frown. ''That's his chronic state, when he isn't married or getting unmarried, that is. I've given up hoping he's ever going to find the right woman…they all seem right to him for the time it takes him to say, 'I do.' But I didn't come here to talk about James. I came because I've heard some amazing stories recently about couples you've brought together, Ilsa, even though I had to do some serious sleuthing to discover the 'professional matchmaker' everyone was whispering about with such reverence was you.''

''I try to keep a low profile,'' she said modestly.

''Appears you're successful on all counts.'' His cup rattled in the saucer as he set one within the other. ''No one would come within a breath of confessing their own *personal* experience, but most all were willing to expound at some length on the miracles you'd wrought for others.''

''I have a knack for recognizing possibilities, perhaps, but that's a far cry from producing a miracle, Mr. Braddock.''

''Please, call me Archer. Gives me a thrill to be on a first-name basis with beautiful women, and these cold winter days, thrills aren't so easy to come by.''

She gave her smile as easily as her acquiescence. "Certainly, Archer."

His nod of approval came on top of his next question. "So, Ilsa, if you're not a miracle worker, how are you able to assist Heaven in making a match between two seeking hearts?"

She set aside her teacup and saucer, finally on solid ground. "I do an extraordinary amount of research," she said. "I study everything I can get my hands on about a person, from old school records to favored hairstyles, preferred leisure activities, favorite and not favorite restaurants, personal convictions and private opinions. I take my time in discovering all I can about a candidate, and then I put all that information aside, and simply pay attention to the world that surrounds my client. Each of us come into contact with an amazing assortment of individuals throughout our lives, but most people aren't paying attention and miss the opportunity to make a connection. I pay attention, and that's why I'm successful. I can provide a list of references, if you'd like, although privacy concerns prevents me from revealing my client list."

"Not necessary," he said. "I did my own research before I made the decision to approach you. Despite the strict confidentiality you request from your clientele, I managed to attain enough information to be considerably impressed. Although I must say, I failed to gain even a glimmer of what you charge for your services. A fact that leads me to believe your fees must be rather substantial."

"It's no simple task to put a price on love, Mr. Braddock." The truth was she charged what she felt her contribution was worth, based on the ability of the customer to pay and her core belief that a genuine ''match'' was worth a genuine sacrifice. ''Could you do it?''

His smile was reflective, wistful, and admiring. ''No,'' he said. ''I would never even try.''

She nodded, glad they agreed.

He nodded, too, then reached into his coat pocket, pulled out a small stack of photographs and handed it to her. ''My grandsons,'' he said with no small degree of pride. ''Adam, Bryce and Peter.''

Ilsa looked at the wallet-size photos one by one, then spread them in a row across the table beside her chair and examined them thoroughly again. Each handsome face was stamped with the same Braddock heritage—strong jaw, straight nose, regal brow—still evident in Archer's aging features and in her own still vivid memory of James's face. The three young men were clearly brothers, although individually quite different. Ilsa had seen their pictures in the society pages and on the cover of the tabloids, of course. The Braddock brothers were favorites of the paparazzi. Their history was the stuff of scandal, and although Ilsa knew only bits and pieces of it, herself, the public knew even less and was hungry for more. It was a testament to Archer and his wife that they had kept the world outside the gates of Braddock Hall, their ancestral home, and raised their three grandsons away from the public eye. But Ilsa could see, even from the two-dimensional photos, that James's sons possessed that indefinable quality that would make them as irresistible to women as Braddock men had been rumored to be for a couple of centuries.

"Very handsome young men," she said, glancing up from the pictures. "Do they have...seeking hearts?"

"Not so anyone could tell," he answered tersely.

Those few words were enough to give her some valuable insight. "But you're their grandfather and you pay attention."

Their eyes met, his still a vivid green, hers a deep and perceptive gray. "Yes," he said. "It's no secret that James has made a hash of finding true love and a game out of marriage and divorce. Janey and I always hoped our grandsons would seek out a relationship similar to our own, one worthy of a lifetime commitment, but not one of them shows a single sign of being capable of recognizing love when it does come along." He pointed out each picture as he named off the brothers. "That's Peter. He's the youngest. He's dazzled by long-legged debutantes. The blue-eyed charmer there in the middle is Bryce. He's our Robin Hood, robbing tomorrow's joys for today's pleasure. He prefers young women with big, toothy smiles and more bosom than brains. The oldest is Adam, who is all business all the time. He's fascinated by any woman who carries a briefcase larger than his."

"Intriguing." Ilsa continued to study the pictures for a moment. "I'm surprised some enterprising mothers haven't solved your matchmaking problems for you long before now."

"Oh, they've tried, believe me. But my grandsons are nearly as slippery as they are suave. It would be a mistake to let them know you and I have even discussed their...future.''

"I am nothing if not discreet, Archer, and I consider myself a facilitator of romance, not an instigator. I initiate a meeting, allow the possibilities to present themselves, then step back and see what happens. Any intervention after that point involves a light touch and great deal of diplomacy.''

"I take that to mean, you don't offer a money-back guarantee.''

"No, but I do have a rather astounding rate of success. If you prefer, your grandsons won't ever know I've been involved in their match. On the other hand, that secrecy requires considerably more effort for the two of us. You'll be my only contact and my best resource for information. Are you sure you won't mind being involved in a somewhat clandestine alliance with me?''

His chuckle came again, rough and charming. "I may be an old man, but I'm not dead yet. My only regret is that Janey isn't here to enjoy this little intrigue along with us.''

"I suspect she has a full-time job being your guardian angel.''

His wrinkled smile turned wistful. "You're right about that.'' He paused, then nodded, clearly ready to close the deal. "So are you up to the challenge of finding the right women for my grandsons?''

"I'm open to the possibilities, yes.'' She met his eyes with a wry smile. "I may never have had three tougher cases, but your grandsons do have a certain cachet to recommend them. The Braddock name will mean something to the young women I introduce to them.''

Archer took a final sip of the coffee, then set his cup and saucer on the table beside his chair and reached for his cane. "It's what the Braddock name means to my grandsons that will cause you the biggest headaches, I'm afraid. But let's not set out on our adventure by worrying about the problems ahead. Let's focus instead on the beginning of a promising new enterprise and the possibility that I might live long enough to see my first great-grandchild.''

Ilsa smiled, very glad to know this was the first of many meetings to come with Archer Braddock. "I'll be in touch in a day or two with a list of information I'll need. The research can take as long as three or four months, but things generally move rather quickly once it's completed. I feel it's very important to be thorough.'' She rose and resisted the impulse to help him up.

He pushed himself out of the chair with only a slight stiffness of movement and shifted his center of balance with the cane. "I have the utmost confidence in you, my dear, but if I may make a small suggestion...begin with Adam. He's the oldest, but I'm also rather worried that he's missed so much in his life. He needs to fall in love with something other than Braddock Industries and he needs to do it very soon.''

"I'll keep that in mind.'' They walked together, slowly but most companionably, to the door and across the foyer. Robert awaited them in the entryway, standing ready with Archer's coat and scarf. "My staff is even more discreet than I am myself,''

Ilsa said. "So you can feel comfortable if you ever need to leave a message with them."

Archer slid his arms into the sleeves of his coat and wrapped the gray scarf around his neck. "Feel free to leave messages for me, too," he said with a wink. "It won't bother me a bit if everyone in my household believes I'm having an illicit affair in my old age." He laughed and looked quizzically at Robert.

"Today is not a good day to be without one's umbrella, sir," Robert said, holding out a black umbrella. "I took the liberty of procuring one for you."

Archer accepted it with an appreciative smile. "Discreet, efficient and exceptionally thoughtful. Thank you, Robert." He turned again to Ilsa. "And thank you, my dear, for a delightful afternoon. I'm looking forward to your call."

Robert prepared to open the door, but Archer paused, holding off the action. "If this works out as we hope, then perhaps you'll consider taking James on as a client."

Ilsa laughed, despite the way her stomach knotted just at the thought. "As I believe we established, Archer, I can't work miracles."

"Ah, well, I think that remains to be seen." And with a tip of his hat, he stepped through the doorway, opened his umbrella, and walked into the drizzly Providence afternoon.

Chapter One

Normally, Adam Braddock steered clear of The Torrid Tomato. The restaurant had found its niche market among the trendy young professionals who spilled from the offices of downtown Providence between the hours of twelve and two, seeking food, fun and a temporary release from stress. Menu items catered to the healthfully eclectic palate, the atmosphere always bordered on boisterous, and over the course of the noon hour, the crowd gravitated toward a high-strung pitch of pandemonium. In Adam's view, the restaurant had just two things going for it on this day in early May: proximity to his office and a noise level that encouraged speedy conclusions to any business, personal or private, being conducted over lunch. As he had no idea why his grandfather had suggested today's meeting with a heretofore unknown old friend of the family, Adam wanted to devote as little time as necessary to it. Hence, his request to meet Mrs. Fairchild at The Torrid Tomato.

She had yet to arrive, and he glanced at the gold Bulgari watch on his wrist, checking the time—ten minutes to twelve—already impatient to be back in the office. The Wallace deal was percolating nicely and he expected a phone call early this afternoon formally accepting the buyout offer. He had a two o'clock appointment with John Selden, the chief operating officer of Braddock Construction, and a three-thirty scheduled with Vic Luttrell, the corresponding executive for Braddock Architectural Designs. At four-forty, he would go over tomorrow's schedule with his administrative assistant, Lara Richmond, and at five-thirty, he would play handball at the club with Allen Mason, Braddock Industries' chief corporate attorney. Tonight he was having dinner with the top two executives of Nation's Insurance Group regarding the possible relocation of their corporate offices to the new Braddock Properties office complex in Boston. All in all, a fairly light day, although he could have skipped lunch entirely and never missed it. But when his grandfather made a request, which he so seldom did anymore, Adam was hard-pressed to find any decent reason to refuse.

A bubbling brook of throaty laughter flowed somewhere behind him, sparkling and effervescent, a lovely sound rising above the frantic noon-hour gaiety. For all its genuine warmth, Adam judged it as a blatant bid for attention from someone, a look-at-me summons to the whole restaurant, and he firmly declined to turn around. All he wanted was a noisy atmosphere, a sort of homogeneous cacophony, nothing overtly distracting…certainly, not the siren's song of amusement that echoed out again as if the laugher couldn't keep it inside. There was something mesmerizing in the lilting tones, something intriguing in the laughter and, despite wanting to ignore the sound altogether, the third time he heard her laugh, he twisted in his chair and craned his neck to see who she might be.

"Adam?"

He whipped back around, chagrined to be caught rubbernecking. "Mrs. Fairchild." He rose with a smile to greet the tall, attractive woman who had spoken, and moved to pull out a chair for her, assessing her age—mid- to early-fifties—her appearance—understated elegance—and the platinum and pearl necklace—genuine, not costume—at her throat, in an appreciative blink. "I'm so pleased you could join me."

"The pleasure is mine." She smiled, extending her hand for a quick clasp of his. The warmth of her greeting held as she took her seat, lifted the folded napkin, and dropped it delicately onto her lap. "Your grandfather speaks so highly of you and your two brothers, I feel I've been remiss in not making more of an effort to get acquainted." She paused, measuring him in a graceful glance. "You are very like James."

"You know my father?"

She nodded. "We were in school together at Exeter and again for a couple of years at Harvard. Well, truthfully, he was two years ahead of me and doubtless never knew I existed. He was always quite charming, though, even during those somewhat awkward adolescent years."

That rang with authenticity. While Adam could never imagine his father as an adolescent, awkward or otherwise, charm was James's calling card, his stock in trade. But Adam was positive his father would have noticed Ilsa Fairchild, no matter what age he might have been at the time. She was very attractive and James Braddock had always had an eye for the ladies. "He would be flattered you remember him, I'm sure."

Ilsa's smile was soft with contradiction. "I'm very taken with this restaurant," she said, neatly shifting the subject. "The atmosphere is always so...energizing. Don't you find it's impossible not to enjoy your meal while surrounded by such joie de vivre?"

Adam had thought it not only possible, but a foregone conclusion. "You've been here before?"

"Several times, although The Torrid Tomato is a fairly recent discovery for me. The first I knew of the restaurant was three months ago, back in February." She looked around, obviously not a bit intimidated by the noise. "But since then, I've developed a rather alarming craving for the artichoke dip. I've been too embarrassed to inquire, but do you suppose they'd sell it by the quart with the reservation of not disclosing the purchaser's name?"

"I'll ask our waiter, if he ever shows up."

Ilsa raised an eyebrow, but didn't otherwise acknowledge his slight show of impatience. "Archer tells me you were barely twenty-five when you became the CEO of Braddock Industries. You must have been the youngest chief executive on record."

"Eight years ago, I was touted as something of a Boy Wonder, but that had more to do with our PR department than any real truth. With all the new technology companies that abound these days and the number of whiz-kids who start their own companies while in college or even high school, I'm practically a dinosaur.''

Ilsa laughed, a pleasant sound that was nearly swallowed up by the din surrounding them. "I can't imagine there are many men of any age who could boast of your accomplishments."

Adam was unimpressed with his own accomplishments. It was the next challenge, the obstacles ahead he found worthy of discussion. "You shouldn't believe everything you hear from my grandfather, Mrs. Fairchild. He's nothing if not biased."

"The facts do seem to support his claims," she said with a gently argumentative smile. "Graduating from Harvard at nineteen—with honors and an MBA—starting out on construction sites so you'd have a comprehensive knowledge of the company and its employees, turning an already successful, commercial construction company into a multibillion dollar conglomerate…. I'd say, your grandfather has every reason to be proud of what you've accomplished."

There wasn't much Adam could—or wanted—to say to that. "You sound like a well-informed shareholder, Mrs. Fairchild."

"And you sound rather modest."

He wasn't modest. He just didn't see anything particularly noteworthy in what he'd done at Braddock Industries. He'd simply updated the good business practices that had guided the family fortunes for over two centuries. "I'm pleased you like what you've learned about the company," he said.

"Hi!" The bright voice bobbed ahead of the slight brunette who dropped into a bouncy squat beside their table. She propped her arms on the table and, with barely a glance at Adam, turned a wide, generous welcome to his companion. "You're usually not here on Tuesdays, Mrs. If. Did you take my advice and get yourself a hot date?" Her eyes were pure blue-bonnet blue, lit with the light of mischief, and Adam felt a jolt of awareness the instant they cut to him. "Hmm," she said, making him feel naked, somehow, under her quicksilver assessment. "A younger man. I approve."

Adam didn't approve at all, but Ilsa merely laughed. "This is Adam Braddock, Katie. A family friend."

Her eyes cut to his again without a glimmer of recognition. "Hi," she repeated, her attention returning instantly to Ilsa. "Guess what? I took your advice."

Ilsa's eyebrows went up in pleasant surprise. "Really? How did that work out?"

The waitress straightened with a bounce, as if she had springs on her feet, lifted her hands above her head and did a dainty pirouette…neatly sidestepping a collision with a waiter who had plates of food balanced from fingertip to shoulder. "Oops," she said, with an unrepentant lift of one shoulder and a flash of smile. "Didn't mean to scare you, Charlie."

The waiter frowned. So did Adam. "Would it be possible to get something to drink?" he asked.

"These are tight quarters, but you get the idea," Katie said to Ilsa.

"All that from one lesson?"

"Two."

"I'm impressed. You may become a ballerina, after all."

"One pirouette after two lessons doesn't exactly qualify me as the teacher's pet."

Ilsa appeared delighted with the exchange and oblivious to the fact that this was a restaurant and this pixie was supposed to be their waitress.

Adam cleared his throat and pitched his voice above the conversational roar in the room...on the generous assumption that the waitress hadn't heard his original request. "I'd like to order now, if that's all right with you."

She looked at him, a wisp of dark hair curling like a wayward ribbon across her cheek, her blue eyes questioning the impatience in his tone. "Well, sure," she said. "But don't you want to peruse the menu first?"

"I've perused," he said, thinking there would be serious consequences—and rightly so—if the manager caught her pirouetting and carrying on lengthy conversations with customers instead of getting their orders. "I'll have the chicken reuben sandwich, no chips, and we'll start with the artichoke dip appetizer." He smiled encouragingly at Ilsa. "What would you like, Mrs. Fairchild?"

She looked thoughtfully from him to the waitress. "I'm going to need a couple of minutes to decide," she said.

"Sure thing," Katie pronounced brightly. "Take your time. I'll find John." Her smile flipped to Adam. Cheeky little thing. He'd have fired her on the spot. "He's your waiter. My tables are over there.'' She tossed her head to indicate the section behind them. "Bye, Mrs. If. Enjoy your…dip.''

She sashayed away, the bounce evident in her light steps, a saucy swing to her hips, a dash of sass in the sway of her long, frizzy ponytail. Halfway through the maze of tables and people, she paused to exchange words with a tall, blond guy—the elusive John, perhaps—and then she laughed, the melodic waterfall of sound drifting back to Adam like the call of the wild.

"She always waits on me when I come in,'' Ilsa said.

"Not today, apparently.'' Adam realized with a start that he'd been staring after the waitress and brought his gaze firmly back under control. Waitstaff should be unobtrusive, efficient without encroaching, friendly, but never personal. The little elf failed on all accounts. "I take it, she's an aspiring dancer?''

Ilsa laughed. "She said she was disenchanted with kickboxing and I suggested ballet as an alternative discipline. I'm actually quite astonished she took a class.''

"Two classes,'' Adam corrected and wondered why he remembered such trivia since the little brunette was now out of sight and nearly forgotten. He seldom, if ever, paid that much attention to the waitstaff in a restaurant like this one. They were, after all, constantly changing and all too often, more intrusive than helpful. He determinedly put her from his mind. "Tell me about yourself, Mrs. Fairchild. My grandfather says you have a small business. A public relations firm, I believe, called…IF Enterprises?''

She did not seem surprised to discover he'd done his research, but then she undoubtedly knew he had employees who did nothing but ferret out such details for him. It was the way he kept abreast of the hundreds of bits of information he needed to know daily. The only way he could survive in his fast-paced, high-stakes world.

"My business is more personal relations than public, although I like to think my endeavors contribute to the overall good of society, too. Everything is related, you know, regardless of how we try to separate one thing from another. Don't you agree, Adam?"

"Absolutely." Adam agreed, his attention already divided. He often tracked two separate and disparate trains of thought at once. It was as natural to him as breathing, and equally essential, in his view. It was a skill he'd learned at an early age by observing his grandfather or perhaps simply by virtue of growing up in an environment where private, public and social lives were so strictly differentiated. He did it without a second thought, he did it extremely well, and he was completely confident Mrs. Fairchild had no idea she wasn't the exact centered focus of his universe at the moment. "Making connections of one sort or another is a big part of what I do every day."

Ilsa smiled. "Me, too."

A waiter arrived. "Hi, my name is John. I'll be your server today." He set two glasses of water on the table and took their lunch order without undue interruption. He was, in Adam's view, a considerable improvement over the ballerina. After that, the conversation drifted into a rather loud, if easy, rundown of mutual acquaintances, society events and who had escorted whom and where. If he hadn't known Mrs. Fairchild was a widow of long standing and had no children, Adam might have believed she had the ulterior motives of a mother with a marriageable daughter. He had plenty of experience in the art of outmaneuvering debutantes and their, ofttimes, forceful mothers. It came with the territory of being an eligible bachelor. But Ilsa seemed not so much interested in his views on matrimony as in what interested him about his life and the society in which he moved. Time and again, she steered the conversation back to him, answering his questions with questions of her own, eliciting his likes, dislikes and opinions he didn't often volunteer. She was skillful in the art of conversation, artful in the way she kept the focus on him, and as she never came within a nuance of getting too personal, he remained perfectly at ease with her.

The appetizer came, accompanied by a fresh peal of the distracting laughter and although he felt the delight of it like the first taste of a good wine, Adam pretended to notice nothing out of the ordinary.

"She has the best laugh in the world." Ilsa said, as if anyone would dare dispute it.

"The pirouetting waitress?" Adam instantly regretted the admission that he'd not only noticed, but had connected the glorious laughter to the bobbing brunette.

Ilsa nodded. "She's a very interesting young woman."

"I'm sure you're right." He didn't doubt Ilsa's assessment, even if he did think it odd for her to take such an interest in a waitress at The Torrid Tomato.

Not that there was anything wrong with being a wait-ress, of course. It was just an unusual friendship for any close family friend of his grandfather's. Cer-tainly not one he, himself, would be inclined to pur-sue. "Are you on the library's fund-raising commit-tee again this year?" he asked, showing that he could turn the topic as adroitly as she.

"It seems to, again, be my turn to chair," she said and from there, the conversation resumed a cadence and content Adam could follow without half trying. At one point, it occurred to him to wonder if Ilsa might be more than just a friend of the family, if she might, in fact, be in the lineup as a future stepmother. But Adam and his brothers had long since given up making predictions about the women who came and went in their father's life and, at the moment, there was already a new fiancée in the picture. Which was not to say Ilsa might not make the running next time around, but if Archer had hopes of introducing her as a potential daughter-in-law, he hadn't expressed that wish to his grandsons. Unless that's what this lunch date had been set up to accomplish. James had never asked his father or his sons for an opinion about his future brides though, so Adam dismissed the speculation from his mind and simply enjoyed the somewhat maternal warmth in Ilsa's smiles and the artichoke dip, which was surprisingly good. He ordered a to-go quart for Ilsa, despite her protests, and wondered aloud if he should check into getting some for Archer's seventy-ninth birthday party.

"You're having a party for him?" Ilsa asked. "Is it a surprise?"

"Only to me," Adam answered with a rueful

smile. "Bryce loves parties and one excuse is as good as another to host one as far as he's concerned. He decided that since Grandfather wouldn't hear of having a party the last two years, we'd celebrate twice as hard this year. Bryce set the day, the time and the magnitude, but working out the details was, as usual, left to me. Peter, my youngest brother, offered to step in and help me out, but he's spending quite a bit of time out of pocket these days, on site at the construction of the Braddock Properties' Atlanta-based operations. Peter's an architect, you know."

She nodded. "I read about him...and the Atlanta project...just recently in the *Providence Journal*."

"I'm very proud of Peter. We all are."

Her smile was warm and genuine. "So the planning of your grandfather's birthday party falls to you, by default."

"Actually, to the party planner of my choosing. Unfortunately, the events coordinator we've used in the past has now officially retired...a direct result, in my opinion, of our last party, when Bryce decided he would handle everything." Adam shook his head, wishing as he always did that his brother would pay a token regard to the small details that comprised a meaningful life. "I keep intending to speak to my secretary about finding someone, but social events have never been high on my priority list and so far, I've forgotten to mention it."

He sipped his water and contemplated whether there was a polite way to make a grab for the last bit of artichoke dip. He decided not to be greedy and realized in the same breath a countermeasure for any hesitancy Wallace might have for accepting the initial offer for his manufacturing company. Despite the noise—unusually rowdy, even for The Torrid Tomato—Adam realized he was enjoying his lunch with Ilsa Fairchild.

"I know an events planner," Ilsa said. "I think you'd like her and she's very dependable. I'll warn you, though, she's extravagantly expensive, but worth every penny. I'll get her name and number for you, if you'd like."

"Great." Adam couldn't help himself. He spread the last of the artichoke dip across the last triangle of toasted bread and popped it into his mouth. Delicious. Maybe he'd been too hasty in his assessment of this restaurant.

"Hi, again." The waitress with the frizzy ponytail returned, dropping into her bouncy squat as if she'd only just vacated the spot. "I just remembered something," she said. To Ilsa. She seemed barely aware Adam was even present at the same table. "The Tai Chi class starts next Monday and you really should call if you're interested. I don't have the phone number with me, but I could bring it to work Thursday, if you're going to be in for lunch."

Ilsa reached for her purse. "Why don't you give me your phone number and I'll call you later to get the information. I'd hate to miss out because the class filled up before I had a chance to call. Would you mind?"

"Not a bit," the waitress said as if the answer was so obvious as to be unnecessary. Then, unexpectedly, her blue eyes came to rest with an unsettling clarity on Adam. "What about you? Any interest in Tai

Chi? It's supposed to be remarkably beneficial for anyone with arthritis or a stiff neck.''

''No, thanks,'' he said coolly, willing the manager to appear and make her go away, wondering if she thought he looked like he needed more exercise. His hand automatically lifted to press against the tense muscles in his neck, then catching himself, he straightened his tie, as if that had been his intent all along. ''I prefer more energetic and competitive forms of exercise.''

She shrugged, a dainty lift of one slender shoulder, and shifted her attention back to Ilsa. ''Got a pencil and paper?'' she asked, as if she wasn't a waitress, on duty, and presumably expected to write down customer's orders from time to time.

Ilsa drew a stylized, misty pink business card from her purse and turned it, blank side up, on the table. ''Just write on that. And thanks so much for reminding me about the class. I'm looking forward to it.''

The little brunette jotted down a phone number and handed back the card. ''I think you'll really enjoy the class. Harry is a wonderful instructor and you won't believe how old he is!'' Her bluebell glance flicked from Ilsa to Adam and back again, challenging them to guess the instructor's age. ''Seventy-four!'' she supplied before any guessing could take place. ''He's a perfect example of why Tai Chi is the very best form of exercise.''

Better than ballet and kickboxing? Adam wanted to ask, but kept his counsel and, instead, took her thinly veiled challenge in stride. He didn't know why he felt anything other than annoyance when he looked at her—she was, after all, a silly little wait-

ress, and not much of one at that—but, however unsettling, he recognized the sparks for the base attraction they were. Not that he could imagine any
circumstances under which he would pursue such an
attraction. And as he felt certain she'd do something
to get herself fired long before he scheduled another
lunch at The Torrid Tomato, it was highly unlikely
he'd ever see her again.

There was a crescendo of noise, the clink and clat-
ter of silverware on glass, and she straightened with
the innate grace of an athlete. "The natives are getting restless," she said, her lips curving with a rueful
smile. "I'm off to assuage their hunger. See you
Monday, if not sooner," she said to Ilsa and moved
past Adam with only a glance to indicate her goodbye. In a moment, the noise died back to a satisfied
chorus of teasing calls and answering laughter...and
Adam experienced a fleeting wish that he were sitting
at a table in the midst of it all, where he could watch
the sparkle in her eyes as she laughed.

"...and the caterer was fit to be tied," Ilsa was
saying, continuing a conversation that Adam had
completely lost the gist of, so absorbed had he been
in the imagined scene going on behind him. He
brought his attention to heel and made sure he didn't
lose focus again.

Outside the restaurant, after they'd finished lunch,
Adam and Ilsa shook hands and exchanged a thank-
you for the meal and the conversation. "I hope to
see you at Grandfather's party," he said. "I can't
promise it will be the best gathering the Braddocks
have ever put together, but if I can get my hands on

an events planner, I intend to make sure she orders plenty of that artichoke dip.''

"In that case, I'll definitely be there,'' Ilsa said with a laugh. "And I will get you the name of that events planner.''

"That would be a help.'' Adam's thoughts were halfway to the office already. "I'll ask my secretary to call you for the information.''

"Or I'll call you. Thanks, again, for lunch. I loved getting to know you a little in person.''

"I enjoyed it tremendously. Take care.'' He waited for her to turn away, which she did, but before he made his own turn in the opposite direction, she was back, extending her hand toward him.

"You might need this,'' she said.

He took it without a glance and slipped it into his suit pocket. "I'll be sure you get an invitation to the party.''

"Perhaps we'll run into each other again in the meantime.'' Then, she walked off at a brisk clip and Adam didn't give her—or the business card she'd given him—another thought.

WHEN THE CARD turned up, Adam barely recalled how he'd come to have it. For nearly two weeks, he'd been immersed in salvaging Braddock Industries' purchase of The Wallace Company and had thought of little else. The deal teetered on the brink of collapse from one day to the next, coming close to agreement and then falling apart all over again. Adam had spent long hours investigating how a "sure thing'' had gone awry, trying unsuccessfully to get Richard Wallace to meet with him, one on one.

So far, Wallace was holding firmly in the negotia-
tions-are-over camp and finally, Adam had sent his
corporate team home for the weekend, telling them
to rest, relax and return with new energy and the
enthusiasm to get this buyout completed, one way or
another.

Adam planned to spend the entire weekend in the
office, coming up with a compromise. For some
months now, Braddock Industries had been quietly
buying up a large chunk of Wallace stock as a negotiating tool but, while Adam had issued the buy
order, he didn't want to initiate a hostile takeover.
Not if there was any other way to get what he
wanted. He admired Richard Wallace tremendously
for building a company out of nothing and, it was
true, Adam's one business failing was his soft spot
for family-run concerns. After all, where would the
Braddock family be if some upstart had decided to
take over the construction business back when it was
vulnerable to such an unwelcome attack? On the
other hand, the offer was a fair one and Adam had
a gut feeling that Richard Wallace had dug in his
heels only because he wanted to walk away with a
little more dignity and considerably more cash than
was first offered.

IF Enterprises, read the raised gold lettering across
the pink card stock. Ilsa Fairchild, 555-5683.

Adam continued to frown at the business card,
newly discovered under piles of reports on his desk.
He recalled his lunch with Ilsa as pleasant, nothing
out of the ordinary, but was still unsure as to why
his grandfather had asked him to meet with her in
the first place. No request for a contribution had been

forthcoming. He hadn't been asked to head up a new fund-raiser for a worthwhile cause. His father's wedding plans were going along apace, and Archer hadn't even asked how the luncheon went or mentioned this old friend of the family since. But then, Adam hadn't been home in the past week and a half, preferring to stay at the Providence apartment and remain focused on the Wallace deal. But now it was Friday night, the staff had long since left for the weekend, and he was staring at a backlog of paperwork…and a misty pink business card.

Turning the card over in his hands, he read the name and phone number written in scrunched and scribbled letters of black ink across the back. Kate— or was it Katie? He couldn't quite make out the letters—Canton. The name meant nothing to him and he wondered why Ilsa Fairchild would have given it to him. But…wait. The birthday party. They'd talked about the birthday party. The one he'd given not a single thought since. Adam vaguely recalled asking Ilsa if she could recommend an events planner. And she'd said…yes? Yes, she did know someone. That must be the reason he'd tucked her card into his pocket and tossed it onto his desk upon his return to the office. She'd written down the name on the back of her business card. He'd intended to give it to Lara, who would have passed it on to Nell, his personal secretary, who would have called this Kate Canton and gotten the party plans underway. But other concerns had pushed the information—and the need for it—out of his mind. Parties were never top priority for him under the best of circumstances.

And now, it was six weeks and counting until

Archer's birthday. Adam realized he'd better take some action…and quickly. A glance at his watch brought a frown. Nine-thirty. Too late to call? Probably he'd get an answering machine, which would be perfect. He could leave a message to call his office Monday morning. Nell would handle everything from there and he wouldn't have to give the matter another thought. Good idea. He dialed the number then began going over yet another financial report on the Wallace Company as he waited for Kate Canton's machine to pick up.

"Hello?"

A person. Adam put down the report, momentarily taken aback. "Kate Canton?" he asked.

"Yes?" Her tone turned cool, cautious.

"This is Adam Braddock."

"Who?"

"Adam Braddock," he repeated. "Ilsa Fairchild gave me your name."

"Why would she do that?"

Okay, so maybe he shouldn't have called after office hours. He warmed his tone to compensate for the suspicious note in her voice. "She thought you might be able to help me. I'm sorry to phone so late in the evening, but I'm in desperate need of a party planner."

"A what?"

Maybe Ms. Canton was a trifle hard of hearing. "A party planner. I need someone to put together a party for me."

"You have the wrong number."

"I don't think so," he said, infusing his tone with the old Braddock charm as he repeated the phone number written on the card, waited for her confirmation, then added, "And you are Kate Canton?"

"Yes, but I'm not a party planner."

Women were so touchy about job titles these days. "Coordinator, then," he said. "Events coordinator. And I mean for this to be quite an event. It's in honor of my grandfather's seventy-ninth birthday at the end of June. There'll be somewhere in the neighborhood of two hundred guests, and—"

"Two hundred," she repeated. "That's a lot of party hats."

She was already calculating expenses. That was a good sign. "I'm sure you're up to the challenge, Ms. Canton. You came highly recommended."

"Someone recommended me to plan your birthday party?"

Hard of hearing and a little thick, too, perhaps. Or falsely modest. Or clever enough to string him along, playing hard to get. Of course, it was also just possible she was simply intimidated by the Braddock name. He'd experienced some strange reactions from people when they realized who he was and the powerful family and fortune he represented. He'd had women hang up on him from sheer nervousness. He'd known some men—and women—to pretend not to recognize the name, as if that somehow put them all on a more level playing field. Whatever Ms. Canton was experiencing, Adam was determined not to lose patience with her. He cleared his throat, dispatching any hint of impatience. "Ilsa Fairchild gave me your name and number and a favorable recommendation."

"Mr. Braddock, you have the wrong number. I

don't know why Mrs. Fairchild gave you my number, but I'm not the person you want.''

Adam frowned. He didn't normally have this much trouble convincing someone to work for him. ''You'll have a free hand with the plans,'' he said persuasively. ''And a very generous budget.''

''Money is not the point,'' she responded quickly.

Money was always the point. ''I realize you must be very busy and may prefer to keep your business centered in Providence, but I can assure you, Ms. Canton, that my family is not without influence in this area, and we do host a number of social events every year. I can't guarantee your business will increase overnight because you do this one party for us, but I believe it is a great opportunity for you. Sea Change is barely a half-hour drive and I'm quite willing to compensate you for any inconvenience. I'll make it well worth your while.''

There was a pause, a considering silence, and Adam relaxed. The tide, he suspected, was turning. ''You're offering me a great opportunity?'' she repeated, a note of humor, a softer touch in her words. ''To plan a party?''

''Yes.'' Ms. Canton was on the hook, ready to make a deal, and Adam was suddenly, resolutely eager to cinch this one. ''I haven't much time and I understand that this is very last minute for you,'' he said. ''So let's cut to the chase. What will it take to get you?''

KATIE COULDN'T DECIDE if she was more offended or flattered that Adam Braddock was so eager to get her. She remembered him from that day at the restaurant, of course, although clearly he didn't remember her. She'd thought he was quite seriously handsome…and quite seriously underimpressed with her. He'd been a bit arrogant for her tastes, way too sure of himself to allow any woman equal footing. Something of a stuffed shirt, actually, and when a smile might have changed her mind, he'd seemed determined to keep frowning. She'd wondered at the time how—and why—the vibrant Mrs. Fairchild had hooked up with him. A family friend, she'd said, which could cover a multitude of sins. People couldn't be held responsible for the friends someone else in their family made. But none of that explained how he'd come to have her phone number. Katie guarded the number of her cell phone—her only concession to practicality and convenience—with a religious zeal and had given it to only a handful of people in the six months she'd been living in Providence. Ilsa Fairchild might have given it out by mistake, but she wouldn't have done so on purpose…not without clearing it with Katie first. And she definitely wouldn't have given her a recommendation as a party planner. No one who knew Katie at all would have done that.

"There's been a mistake, Mr. Braddock," she began. "I'm not the person you meant to call."

"Please, Ms. Canton, don't be coy. I'm a busy man. The party's only six weeks away and I don't have the time or the inclination to track down another coordinator. Name your price and let's get this settled."

His tone was so serious, his manner so "Let's Make a Deal" that Katie wanted to laugh. What kind of man got so worked up over a birthday party? A busy man. A man who made lists and marked off items with a superior sense of self-satisfaction. A man with a singular mind-set, who was completely determined to refute her every denial. ''Five thousand dollars,'' she said, positive he'd hang up on her faster than she could say…just kidding.

''Done.''

Katie swallowed her laughter like a big wad of chewing gum. ''What?'' she choked out.

''You said five thousand. I agreed.''

She thought fast. ''You didn't let me finish. It's five thousand now and another five thousand later.'' There, that should fix his wagon.

He did hesitate. ''You must be very good, Ms. Canton. For that price, I'll expect you to plan a beautiful June day into the bargain. Phone my secretary tomorrow…no, Monday morning, and she'll make arrangements to get a deposit check to you. You'll want to make a preliminary visit to Braddock Hall and look over the estate. Nell—my secretary—will make those arrangements as well. Just tell her when you'll be driving down and she'll take care of everything. Any questions?''

Are you crazy? But when Katie found her voice, she just managed to squeeze out a croaky, ''I don't drive.''

That seemed to slow him down. For about two seconds. ''Then I'll send the Rolls for you. Nell will work out the day and time with you.''

The Rolls. He would send ''The Rolls'' for her. Over the span of her twenty-six years, Katie had been the recipient of bus tickets, cab fares, carriage rides, even a first-class plane ticket once. But no one had ever before said, "I'll send The Rolls for you," as if it was the obvious, only thing to be done. "The Rolls?" she repeated.

"The chauffeur is Benson. He'll take you anywhere you want to go. Within reason, of course."

A Rolls-Royce with a chauffeur. Benson, the chauffeur. Anywhere she wanted to go. Within reason, of course. Of course. But it was tempting—more than tempting—to say, "hey, sure thing, send it on." How often did a person get offered such an adventure? On the other hand, she wasn't crazy enough to think any of this would happen. "Well," she said. I'll certainly look forward to that."

"Good. I'll tell Nell to expect your call."

Katie sighed, wishing for the first time that Adam Braddock hadn't gotten her number by mistake. "Yes, well, thanks for calling. Bye, now."

"Ms. Canton?"

The authority in his voice caught her before she could hang up. "Yes?"

"You'll need my office number."

"Oh, right."

He gave it to her in clipped, no-nonsense terms. "Got that?"

Right. "Sure thing," she said.

"You'll call Monday, and ask for Nell."

"Nell." Katie wrote the name in the air beside the phone number and watched it disappear. "Got it."

"Good. Nell will get the particulars to you…date, time, guest list." He paused.

Katie thought he must be realizing his mistake. "Having second thoughts?" she asked cheerfully.

"No. I was wondering if I should arrange to meet with you myself."

"I know a great little restaurant downtown. The Torrid Tomato." Her smile curved in delightful anticipation of that meeting. "I could meet you there practically any day at noon."

"No, that won't be necessary," he said hastily. "I'm sure you'll work out just fine."

Okay, now she was offended. "Mr. Braddock," she began in earnest…and was immediately interrupted.

"Adam," he corrected. "And shall I call you Kate?"

"I prefer Katie." No one but her dad had ever called her Kate, and she'd just as soon keep it that way. Not that Adam Braddock was apt to be calling her anything close to her name once he realized he'd offered a waitress ten thousand dollars—and the use of his Rolls-Royce—to plan a birthday party. "And we should probably stick with Mr. Braddock and Ms. Canton. Keep things strictly business, you know."

She could imagine his frown. Adam Braddock was accustomed to getting his way. "Whatever you think, Ms. Canton. I'll tell Nell to expect your call, first thing Monday morning."

Katie let her widening smile carry over into her voice, coloring her words with the good humor that invariably accompanied her sense of the ridiculous. "Sure thing, Mr. Braddock. And, really, thanks a million for calling. Yours is the best offer I've received in months."

Then she clicked off the cell phone, certain that was the last she'd be hearing from Adam Braddock.

Chapter Two

The cell phone rang just as Katie walked out the front door of Hair Today, Gone Tomorrow. She'd chosen the salon because it was only a short walk from the bus stop and because the name struck her as funny. And appropriate. In a couple of weeks she'd be gone, on her way to another place, a change of scene, the next new adventure of her life. She liked Providence, could see herself spending a year or two or three or more here. But the longer she stayed, the harder it would be to leave and there were other cities she wanted to experience, other places she wanted to see. Moving around was the way she exercised her restless spirit and kept her personality on its toes. It was the way she celebrated the lives of the family she'd lost, the way she made amends for being the only survivor. Change was always a positive in her opinion, a necessary discomfort, and in deference to that creed, her hair was gone...well, a lot of it, anyway.

The phone rang again and she pulled her curious fingers away from the springy cap of natural curls to reach into her bag for the phone. The Caller ID read Unavailable, but in some cities, the listing agency's number came up that way and since she was expecting a call from Caroline about a house-sitting job in Baton Rouge, Katie clicked on, expecting to hear a familiar Mid-western accent. "Hello?"

"Ms. Canton?"

Definitely not Caroline—the tones too crisp and rounded—but perhaps someone else in the office. "Yes?"

"My name is Nell Russell. I work for Adam Braddock, Braddock Industries. Mr. Braddock asked me to call and arrange a time for your visit to Braddock Hall this week. He mentioned he'd spoken with you about it on Friday."

Katie blinked, a bit taken aback by the way the woman's voice fairly vibrated with importance every time she said *Braddock*. And she'd said it a lot in that five-second introduction. "As a matter of fact, he did—"

"Mr. Braddock said that if you hadn't phoned by nine-thirty this morning, I was to reach you at this number and set up a time for Benson to drive you to Sea Change. I know it's already ten, but I did want to catch you before you left your office for lunch."

Katie glanced at the traffic buzzing past, the deli on the corner, the bank across the street, and opened her mouth to say she didn't have an office. Or have need of one.

"I can arrange a time to call back later today, if it would be more convenient," Ms. Russell continued, her voice picking up speed. "But Mr. Braddock was very specific in his instructions. It's important that we arrange a time this week for you to visit

Braddock Hall. It's only a little over six weeks until Mr. Archer Braddock's birthday, as I'm sure you are aware, and the sooner we get this trip scheduled, the sooner you can get your plans underway for the party.''

Katie plunged in before the last syllable cleared the airwaves. ''I'm afraid there's been a mistake. You see, Mr. Braddock called the wrong—''

''I understand completely,'' Nell said, demonstrating that she didn't listen any better than her employer. Or maybe she wasn't programmed to accept any possibility that the name, *Braddock,* and the word, *mistake,* could occur in the same conversation. ''I know you're very busy, Ms. Canton, and I'll be brief. I've been instructed by Mr. Braddock to put Benson and the Rolls at your disposal and accommodate your schedule for any day this week you're available. If it would be of any assistance at all, I'm certain Mr. Braddock wouldn't mind if I helped make the calls necessary to shift your appointments and clear some time on your calendar. So is tomorrow possible for you? Or the day after?''

Katie stepped to the curb, out of the flow of pedestrian traffic, and pressed the phone closer to her ear to cut some of the noise. Although why she should be trying so hard to hear, was difficult to say. A chance to explain the misunderstanding didn't appear to be on the agenda as Nell Russell barely paused for breath. ''Thursday would work almost as well as tomorrow, but Friday is late in the week and the traffic is just terrible and with Mr. Bryce Braddock and Mr. Peter Braddock home for the weekend,

I'm afraid you'll run into more distractions than earlier in the week, but if that's the only day you can schedule the visit, we will, of course, accommodate you.''

There was a pause, and Katie jumped in, her sense of the ridiculous rising to the occasion. It wasn't as if anyone was listening to what she said anyway. ''As luck would have it, today's my only free day, so you see, I won't be able to make that trip after all.''

''Today might work,'' Nell said, a lightbulb of possibility going off in her voice. ''Hold a moment, please.''

Faster than Katie could backtrack and say, *Oh, wait, today won't work,* she was on hold and wondering why she hadn't specified that today wasn't even up for consideration. She should just hang up. But Adam Braddock had no doubt instructed his secretary to keep calling until Katie agreed to go.

So why didn't she? Agree to go, that is. It was her day off and she'd never been to the town of Sea Change, never even heard of it until Adam's call. She'd never been invited to tour a house with a name, either. That might be fun. Plus, there was the ride in the Rolls to sweeten the temptation.

''Ms. Canton?'' Nell was back. ''Are you in town, now?''

Hard to deny, since the traffic noise was all around her. ''Yes, but—''

''Wonderful. If you'll give me your directions, Benson will pick you up within the next thirty minutes, drive you to the estate and bring you back this evening. I'm so glad this has worked out. Mr. Braddock would be most upset if we'd failed to make this connection. He's anxious for you to see Braddock Hall. It's a lovely place and I'm sure you'll enjoy the drive down, as well as touring the grounds. This is a good time for you, then?''

Katie debated with her conscience. She would be going under false premises, true. But she hadn't misled anyone and she had tried to correct the misunderstanding. While only a precocious preteen, she'd adopted the physicians' creed of First, Do No Harm as her own...and really, what harm could there be in her going for a drive with Benson in the Rolls? Adam Braddock was no closer to finding a legitimate party planner whether she took a ride in his car or not. And she could always figure out some way to pay Benson for the gas. She knew she'd regret not taking the chance and, when all was said and done, her main goal in living was to end every day with as few regrets as possible.

''Now is the perfect time for me,'' she said, decision made. ''Tell Benson, I'll be waiting on the corner of—'' She glanced up at the street signs, ''Weybosset and Orange whenever he arrives. And thank you.'' Katie clicked off the phone, dropped it into the depths of her bag, and gave her new crop of curls a saucy toss to shake off the nagging voice of reproach.

Okay, so she could have, probably should have, tried harder to explain. But life was short and she'd vowed to experience all that it offered with her chin up, and her hopes high. She owed that much to the family she'd lost so long ago that she couldn't even remember their smiles. She owed that much and more to the lost little girl she once had been. To live every moment as if it were a gift was the only promise she'd ever made to herself...and right or wrong, she was taking a ride in Adam Braddock's Rolls-Royce. She was going to enjoy every moment of the experience, too. And if tomorrow it still seemed necessary, she'd do her penance by looking up party planners in the Yellow Pages and phoning Nell with a selection of names and phone numbers. It was the least she could do.

Someone in the milling crowd jostled her as the light changed from Don't Walk to Walk. As people moved past her into the crosswalk, busy with their own agendas, she backed up to the wall of the building on the corner and allowed her lips a whimsical grin. Anticipation bubbled inside her, and she felt a little sorry for anyone who wasn't her, standing on the corner of Weybosset and Orange, waiting for the Rolls to come for her.

SO MUCH FOR ANTICIPATION, she thought as she stepped into the back of the silver-gray automobile and came face-to-face with Adam Braddock. What the heck was *he* doing here? And what would she say when he demanded to know what a *waitress* was doing climbing into his Rolls-Royce?

"Ms. Canton? I'm Adam Braddock," he said, glancing up and extending his hand over the top of the small computer on his lap. "So nice to meet you."

"Hello," she said, realizing he hadn't recognized her. Yet. The door closed behind her with a sturdy *ka-thud* and as it was too late to make a run for it, she settled onto the seat with a soft, leathery *sshh-plop,* and returned his solid handshake with a limp-wrist brush of her fingers. "Nice car."

His handsome face barely registered a vague smile before his eyes were back on the computer screen. "I'm glad you were able to make the trip to Braddock Hall on such short notice."

"I, uh, wasn't expecting to see you."

"It's an unexpected trip." He frowned at the computer screen and typed in a response.

Katie fidgeted on the seat, wishing he'd recognize her and get it over with, thinking this car seat was made of the softest leather ever to come into contact with her own seat, wondering if there was any way she could get out of this situation gracefully. "Sort of unexpected or really unexpected?"

"What?" His tone barely made it a question, his eyes didn't stray from the screen.

"Well, if it's *sort of* unexpected, like a broken water heater, then this probably isn't the best time for me to visit and we ought to just reschedule, but if it's *really* unexpected, like someone in the family has appendicitis, then I should just get out of the car now and let you make the trip by yourself."

"No." His voice for all its vagueness, sounded pretty authoritative. "That isn't necessary."

But Katie wasn't giving up on escape that easily. "But if someone's ill—"

"Christmas decorations," he said succinctly.

"What?"

"Christmas decorations," he repeated, displaying not a single other sign he realized she was sitting beside him in the car.

"Christmas...in May?"

He picked up a phone—conveniently positioned in the door console—and punched in a number. One number, rapid dial. Naturally. "Lara," he said sharply into the phone. "The stock's moving. Any word from Wallace?"

He listened so intently Katie could all but feel the energy of his thoughts. He was as smoothly controlled as the car in which they were riding and exuded the same sort of luxuriant power. Harnessed. Refined. But there was frustration beneath the surface, and it was a quite incredibly perfect surface, too. His dark hair was cut with the precision of a master stylist, not too short, not too long, not a hair out of place. Perfect from every angle. His clothes, too—a dark gray suit, white shirt, exemplary tie, right down to the Windsor knot—reflected a pristine attention to detail. His profile—almost the only angle she had been shown since she got in the car—revealed the same strong, even features as a face-on view. In other words, perfect. She'd thought he was attractive in the restaurant, of course, but here in his natural habitat, he was quite extraordinarily handsome. Even better to look at than the Rolls...and that was saying something. Katie leaned back against the supple leather seat and watched him in profile, deciphering from his intense expression and his silence that he was capable of listening when he wanted to do so. Or when he was interested. What would it be like, she wondered, to have a man like Adam Braddock focus that same intensity on her? What would it take to engage his interest?

Of course, when he realized she was a waitress at The Torrid Tomato and not the events planner he'd hired, sight unseen, for an exorbitant amount of money, she just might find out. She figured he'd be angry with her, even though the fault was largely his. No doubt he had yes-women at his beck and call, in the office and out of it, too, and she didn't imagine he ever took kindly to hearing explanations. It was too much to ask of perfection, she supposed, to expect him to entertain the idea that had he only listened to her for two minutes in the first place, she wouldn't be in his car right now.

Okay, so it was her own choice to be in the car. She couldn't exactly blame him for that. But still he ought to be gentlemanly enough to share some of the responsibility.

"Good work, Lara. Remember, as far as Wallace knows, I'm unavailable the rest of the week. Let's see if he doesn't break a sweat by this time tomorrow." He hung up without another word. No goodbyes necessary with Lara, apparently. Or perhaps he was already so engrossed in the activity on his little computer screen he didn't know he hadn't given a polite "over-and-out" to the conversation. That made more sense, she decided, as he didn't seem to remember he wasn't alone, either.

Katie fidgeted a little more, wondering what it would take to persuade him to look up from that computer. Conversation, clearly, wouldn't. And she didn't give a simple, straightforward request much of a shot, either. Even if he were polite enough to pretend an interest in any discussion she proposed, she'd receive barely half of his attention. At best. Studying his intense and concentrated expression, Katie doubted he'd notice if she stripped naked and tossed her clothes out the window. Maybe if she started with her shoes and aimed them at his window…or at him? But the way her luck was running so far, she'd probably just hit him in the head with her Birkenstock sandal and knock him unconscious. Which wouldn't be much of an improvement.

Plus, there was probably some law against being barefoot—much less naked—in a Rolls-Royce… whether the owner noticed or not. She tapped her feet on the lush carpet of the floorboard, wished she'd worn her Old Maine Trotters instead of the sturdy sandals, even though she had just treated herself to a pedicure at the beauty salon. She wiggled her toes and wondered if she would be admitted to the pretentious-sounding Braddock Hall in her denim jumper and red T-shirt or if some haughty butler would quietly suggest she slip on a jacket and tie or send her around to the back door. Shifting her backpack purse to the seat beside her, she wished her phone would ring, so she could demonstrate to Adam Braddock that she was no more focused on him than he was on her. He might even enjoy eavesdropping on her conversation. It was possible he was simply shy and lacking in social—as well as listening— skills. She cut a sidelong glance to him and sighed, again. What was she thinking? The man practically had skills oozing out of every pore. And she had no doubt he could turn on considerable charm when it occurred to him to do so. Why would she think for two seconds that she could best him in a dueling phones scenario? He'd have her on the mat before the second ringy-ding-ding.

She subdued yet another sigh and turned to gaze out the window, but the Rolls, for all its seamless negotiation, had yet to pull away from the city landscape and there was nothing much to see. Unless she counted the way the smoky tint on the glass shaded the outside world, turning the sky and everything under it muted and pale, while enclosing her in a serene bubble of privacy and soft, soothing color. Even the music drifting like a slight breeze around her was meant to be unobtrusive and formless, a background for Braddock business conducted while traveling from one office to another. There was even a glass partition between the back seat and Benson, which precluded learning anything about him, except that the back of his silver head wasn't that fascinating. Her gaze sidled over to see what she could see on the computer screen and as that proved to be not much, her body followed, sliding gradually into a forty-five degree angle where she could just begin to make out the data on the computer. Numbers. Lots of…

"Are you interested in the stock market, Ms. Canton?"

She tried to be as graceful as possible while sliding

back to an upright position. "Isn't everyone these days? And you can call me Katie."

His eyebrows went up slightly and a glimmer of amusement lit his whiskey-brown eyes for a second. "I thought we were going to keep our association strictly business," he said.

"Oh, we are." She gave him one of her best mystery smiles—all lips, no teeth. Not that he noticed. "But since we're sharing a ride and presumably some conversation along the way, it'll be easier if we dispense with the mister and ms. stuff."

"Hmm." His glance flicked over her, lingering on her glistening—thanks to the new haircut and a new Aveda product—hair and with a sinking sensation, she knew any minute now he'd be tossing her out on her waitress butt. But with only a faint and fleeting frown, his gaze cut back to the laptop. "Have you made any plans for my grandfather's birthday, Katie?"

If he'd had any recognition of her at all, it was gone with the latest shift in the Dow Jones. She was beginning to think the challenge was not in getting out of this situation with grace, but in getting him to notice she was in it in the first place. "I thought maybe I'd get him a tie. What about you?"

The slight lift of his mouth showed that he wasn't completely without a sense of humor. "I'm thinking along more practical lines. A small manufacturing company."

"That's going to take a lot of wrapping paper."

"Good thing I own stock in Hallmark." Again he

tapped keys on the keyboard. "I meant, of course, what plans you may have made for the party."

"I'm only going to see the house," she said candidly. "I haven't given the party a single thought."

His frown might have been for her. Then again, maybe not. "That's commendable," he said.

"It is?"

His eyes stayed on the screen. "You haven't wasted your creative energy making plans that could easily be thrown askew by logistics."

"No, indeed," she agreed. "Because, of course, no one likes to be thrown askew." She was rewarded with a sidelong glance and smiled to herself. "I mean, who knows when Christmas decorations are going to pop up and cause unexpected trips right smack in the middle of a perfectly pleasant May?"

He pursed his lips slightly as the flow of data blinked and rolled across the computer screen. "Sea Change is a small town by anyone's standards," he said. "It's neither by the sea nor particularly adaptable to change. Any change. Replacing the old, worn-out Christmas decorations has turned into a major undertaking, with half the town council voting to duplicate the original designs and the other half insisting on a more modern theme and everyone else disagreeing in general. Unfortunately, compromise isn't a word much used in our town and as I'm currently chairman of the town council, I've been summoned to an emergency meeting to decide the issue." His fine brown eyes met her blue ones, and her silly heart skipped a beat. "Isn't that what you wanted to know, Katie?"

Okay, so it skipped two beats. Possibly three, altogether. Which only proved she was as susceptible to a handsome face as the next woman. "I was curious, yes. You're obviously a busy man and well, Christmas decorations didn't seem important enough to lure you out of your office. I thought you were just being evasive. Which is fine. It's certainly none of my business why you're making the trip to Sea Change. Today." *Of all days.*

His attention and his gaze unsettled her in equal measures, but his sudden smile made her glad she'd gotten out of bed this morning. "No need to worry, Katie. I won't get in your way."

She laughed because that was so clearly implausible. "Too late."

Surprise lent a slight crinkling around his eyes, a gentler cast to his smile. "So you do have some plans in mind, after all." He nodded, seeming satisfied that she was doing her job. "Commendable."

Apparently, she could do no wrong—as long as she was doing what he wanted done. "You're easier to please than I expected. I'm commended if I don't make any plans and commended if I do make them but just don't want you to know I've made them."

"I trust people to do what's expected of them in their own way and without my supervision."

"That's a very optimistic attitude."

"It's simply the only way to delegate authority. I don't have the time or inclination to plan a party. That's why I hired you and, as long as my grandfather has a good time, you have carte blanche to plan the party in any manner you see fit."

"Oh good, then the belly dancers are a go."

His smile slid into a patient amusement and his gaze slipped back to the computer. "He'll be seventy-nine and he is in good health, but let's not push the envelope."

"Gotcha," she said as if making a note to herself. "Fun, but conservative. Dancing in, bellies out. Any other restrictions on this carte blanche you've given me?"

"Only that you exercise good taste."

"Oh, well, if *that's* a requirement, you'll definitely need to find someone else."

There was a flicker of amusement in his eyes, a touch of humor in his solemn tones. "I'm glad to know you have a sense of humor, Katie, and I have the utmost faith in your judgment. I also trust you're aware that a few words from me can greatly enhance your reputation. Or severely cripple it. It really is in your own best interest to ensure this party comes to pass without a hitch."

"Or a belly flop," she said, wondering how he managed to stuff that much ego into his nice white shirt without getting either one wrinkled. "I think you can rest assured, Mr. Braddock, that I—"

"Adam," he corrected absently, his attention circling back on that dumb computer screen.

"Adam," she repeated dutifully, wishing his name didn't feel so weightless and welcome in her mouth. "Rest assured I have no intention of—"

The phone rang then, a distracting *tweet* of a noise, and he had it to his ear in a flash. In less than a second, she was forgotten, relegated to a blip in the background of his consciousness.

"Yes, I see it," he said, staring intently at the computer screen. "He's a fool if he holds out much longer. He'll lose everything. I haven't a clue what he thinks he can gain by this. Put Allen on."

Katie listened—as if she could do anything but—while the one-sided conversation filled up with legal terms and contract points. A year or more ago, she'd worked in a Seattle brokerage firm for a few months and picked up enough of the lingo to recognize that Braddock Industries was conducting a surefooted and leveraged buyout. So Adam *was* getting his grandfather a manufacturing company for his birthday. Imagine that.

"He can't afford to be that obstinate. What is he thinking?" He snapped the words into the phone, but even Katie could tell it was a rhetorical question. No answer except the one he wanted would ever satisfy Adam Braddock. "Wallace can't expect we're going to make a better offer."

"He's concerned about his employees," Katie said, hardly aware she'd spoken her thoughts aloud, much less expecting to get any response to her unsolicited opinion.

"What did you say?" Adam's sharp tone brought her up short. "No, Allen," he continued. "I was asking Katie...the events planner."

She gave a guilty start and realized she suddenly had his full and complete attention. "Me?"

"What did you just say?"

Offering another, now rather nervous, mystery

smile, she gave a little shrug and repeated hesitantly, "He's concerned about his employees?"

Adam frowned, his gaze probing hers, a muscle flexing in his jaw, his concentration all on her and yet somewhere far away, too. The sheer energy of his thoughts seemed to pulse in the air around her and echo in the sound of her quickening heartbeat. In the future, she would be a little more careful about what she wished for. But then as unexpectedly as it had come, his focus shifted back to the computer screen and the person on the other end of the phone. "Let me talk to Lara." The pause was barely discernible, before he was issuing instructions. "Sweeten the deal for the employees," he said. "Job guarantees, severance packages, whatever inducements you think will get Wallace and his team to the table. I want this done right and I want it done now."

If Lara voiced anything other than swift obedience, she had wasted her breath because he clipped the phone back in the console almost before the last words were out of his mouth. "How did you know that?" he asked.

Katie lifted her chin, determined to remain unintimidated by his brusque intensity. "I couldn't exactly help overhearing your conversation."

He waved that away with an impatient hand. "What made you say what you did about the employees?"

"I worked in a Seattle brokerage house for a while and I heard a lot of talk around the water cooler about a big merger that fell through because the president of the smaller company didn't feel his employ-

ees were being given enough respect by the CEO of
the big corporation. No one could believe the guy
would give up several million dollars to protect his
employees, but he did.'' She shrugged. ''Listening
to your conversation made me remember, that's all.''

''I should have thought of that possibility myself,''
he said, sounding rather astonished that he hadn't and
she had. ''Someone on my team certainly should
have. I can't believe we've spent two weeks beating
our heads against the wall and, out of the blue, you
nail the problem.''

''It was only a thought,'' she said, not exactly flattered by his disbelieving tone. ''I could be wrong.''

''If you are, Braddock Industries stands to lose a
substantial investment of time and money.''

Sure thing. As if he'd take any risk based solely
on her opinion. ''In that case, if I'm right, you'll owe
me a substantial steak dinner. Dessert, too. And FYI,
I prefer ice cream. None of that yogurt masquerading
as ice cream. I like the real deal.''

He tipped his head to the side, regarded her with
a slow devastating smile. ''Are you asking me out
for dinner?''

Whoa. Not her intention, at all. ''Don't toy with
me, Adam. You'll spoil my image of you.''

''Do you think I wouldn't let a woman take me
out for dinner?''

''Of course you wouldn't. You don't go out to
dinner. You eat meals at your desk or in the car, in
between phone calls and market updates. I'll bet you
and Benson are regulars at the McDonald's drive-
thru.''

His laugh was even nicer than his smile. "You have a vivid imagination, which must be an asset in your line of work."

"Yes," she said, feeling ever more hopeful she wasn't going to find herself thumbing rides to get back home. "It's also something you may want to remember in case you need an outside opinion on the Great Christmas-Decoration Debate."

"Trust me, you don't want to get mixed up in that. Sea Change doesn't take kindly to the opinions of outsiders. That's what's caused most of this trouble in the first place."

Katie opened her mouth to reply, but the phone tweeted again, and she lost what little ground she might have gained. But then, why was she trying to gain anything with this guy? There was no place for an attraction—and she did admit there were a few elemental sparks of that zinging around in the back of the Rolls-Royce—to go. And what could possibly happen? She was a rolling stone. He was moss. She had a lot of living to do. He had a lot of phone calls to make. He was as out of her league as she was out of his. Teasing him, trying to lure him into showing some interest in her would only hasten her fall from grace and result in a long walk back to town. They were so far out of the city now, she doubted she could find a bus to catch if she waited all day. Better for her, if she ignored him and his conversations and just looked out the window as the cityscape changed to a soft, spring-green countryside. It was a much more realistic approach, too, considering that he was already communing with the computer and the phone, and was once again wholly oblivious to her presence beside him.

"WELL, WHERE IS SHE?" Adam glanced at his watch before scanning the bustling town square of Sea Change, Rhode Island, wondering where Katie Canton could be.

"I don't know, sir." Benson rubbed the base of his ear with one hand and adjusted the brim of his chauffeur's cap with the other. "She was out of the car so fast, by the time I came around to open the door she was already gone."

"I was only gone fifteen minutes," Adam said, glancing at his watch. "Why did she think I suggested she wait in the car?" He had spent his life being responsible, doing what he was supposed to do, taking care of business. He didn't go gallivanting off every time there was a fifteen-minute window of opportunity. And he always told someone where he was going and how he could be reached. He did not have time to chase down an errant party planner, but it didn't appear that he had any choice. "She didn't say anything before she got out of the car? Nothing to indicate where she was going?"

"She said she wanted to get a feel for the town," Benson replied. "That's all, sir. Just a feel for the town."

Adam sighed. "Wait here, Benson. I'll find her." And he strode up Dockside Avenue to do so.

A half hour later he ran her to ground in Belle's Book Nook, sitting behind the cherrywood bank teller's cage Belle used as a desk and chatting up a blue streak with Belle's daughter, Rorie Ann.

"Well, speak of the devil and look who walks in." Rorie flashed a smile reckless with welcome, then she leaned across the polished cherrywood, providing him with a good view of her cleavage. In one form or another, Adam had been receiving the same smile—and as often as not, the same view—from the nubile daughters of Sea Change for almost as long as he could remember. He was always careful to return the smile with the proper balance of warmth and discouragement. The view he tried to ignore completely. Any other response was dangerous. Not so long ago, one of the tabloids had run a front-page story on Bryce's secret elopement with one of the local young women. The report was blatantly false, the grainy photos obviously doctored, and a few words from Archer, in the form of a legal threat, had resulted in a stilted apology. But somehow that never seemed to allay the gossip. So Adam was careful. Always. And he advised his brothers, however futilely, to be cautious, too. "Hello, Rorie Ann," he said with a careful smile.

"Hel-lo, Adam." She stretched the words into several seductive syllables and barely let her glance cut to Katie. "This is Adam Braddock. The one I was telling you about, Katie. Adam, this is Katie Canton."

"We've met." He resisted the urge to consult his watch and thereby, make Katie aware she was causing an unnecessary delay. "In fact, she's the reason I'm here." Ignoring the swift reassessment in Rorie's expression, he smiled amiably at Katie. "I've been looking for you. Benson had no idea where you had gone."

"You know each other?" Rorie clearly was calculating all she'd divulged in however long the women had been chatting and trying to recall if she'd said anything she might not want repeated. "We were just talking about the Christmas decorations," she said, swiftly allying herself with Adam and the rest of the Braddocks. "I was telling her that this town isn't going to put up a bunch of gaudy, tinsel reindeer just because a *few* people have no taste."

Adam was weary of the argument already, and he'd only been in town long enough to mediate a fifteen-minute feud between Mayor Henry and Councilwoman Browning. And, of course, the thirty minutes he'd spent listening to various other complaints as he'd hurried in and out of the shops, searching for his missing party planner. "We should be going, Katie," he said impatiently, even though it was not yet noon. "The day is getting away from us and you'll want to see the Hall in natural light."

Rorie frowned at her new confidant, surprise etched all over her pretty face. "You're going with him? To the Hall?"

Katie unfolded herself from the chair with the leisurely grace of a dancer. Or a kickboxer. "He didn't give me much choice," she said with a playful smile. "The man all but kidnapped me this morning."

"Kidnapped?" Rorie's eyes rounded with curiosity as her gaze swivelled to him. "Really?"

"She's here to take a look around the Hall," he

explained, knowing the propensity of the town grape-vine to turn anything he did into something it wasn't. Next thing he knew, the tabloids would have him kidnapping women for sport. "Katie is in charge of planning Grandfather's birthday party next month."

Rorie turned to Katie, accusation in her eyes. "You didn't mention that."

"I'm sorry." Katie sounded honestly sincere. "I didn't know it was important."

Now that was a bit cavalier, Adam thought, even for the casual Ms. Canton. "More so to some than others." He matched her nonchalance, knowing Rorie would miss the undertone, and that Katie wouldn't.

"Thanks for the recommendations." Katie came around the teller's cage with a canvas bag stuffed to the brim with books.

He automatically reached to take the bag, but her frown warned him away.

"I'll carry them, thanks." She hefted the bag into her arms, bowing a little with the weight.

"It's heavy," he said, making another, chivalrous attempt to relieve her of the burden.

She swung her armful of books out of reach. "Honestly, I prefer to carry them myself. It's part of the experience of buying a book, you know. The weight of it in your hands. The anticipation of open-ing it when you're alone."

"Doesn't the anticipation of so *many* at one time strain the experience?"

She flashed a smile, then added a conciliatory, "No, but thanks for your concern, anyway." Turning sideways, she squeezed between him and a tall shelf marked American Literature, 20th Century, the bulging sack pulling at his suit jacket as she crawfished past, the warmth of her touching him in passing, a soft jasmine scent catching him unaware with its pleasure. "Bye, Rorie," she called. "It was great meeting you."

"Same here." Rorie said, although she didn't sound too sure of it. "See you at the meeting this afternoon, Adam."

"Wouldn't miss it," he said, even though he'd rather do practically anything else. But he'd be there, of course. As soon as he'd dropped Katie off at the Hall and checked some figures in his office there. He'd prefer to be in Providence, of course, but as chairman of the town council, he had an obligation to attend the meeting and arbitrate some kind of peace. One way or another, Braddocks had been mediating the battles of Sea Change since the town was founded by the first James Braddock in 1805. Taking part in local matters was a family tradition and Adam wasn't about to be the first Braddock in nearly two hundred years to cast Sea Change politics adrift in a stormy sea of conflict and indecision, no matter how much he'd like to.

With a nod and a smile for Rorie, he followed Katie's overladen progress toward the door, trying to see over her shoulder to read, at least, the top title of her purchases. *Louisiana Myths,* it looked like, although he couldn't be sure the way she bobbed and weaved around tables and shelves, toting the weight of all that anticipation. "What are you going to do with all those books?'' he asked, wondering if he'd be allowed to open the door for her, or if struggling with the knob was a part of the book-buying experience, too. ''Once you're alone with them, that is.''

''Read them.'' She glanced at him over her shoulder. ''Then give them to someone else to read. What do *you* do with books?''

''I get someone else to carry them whenever possible.'' He reached past her and pushed open the door, an action she met with a mysterious sort of smile. He found himself smiling back, stupidly pleased to be able to do something for her. Then, just as swiftly, he remembered the time she'd cost him already today and was annoyed that she didn't seem to know, or care, he'd had to spend the better part of a half hour tracking her down. He was annoyed she wouldn't let him carry the books she'd bought. He was even annoyed by the carefree bounce of her dark curls. There was something familiar about that. About her. A fleeting thought that he'd seen her somewhere before. A Providence party, most likely.

''I see you found some books, Ms. Canton.'' Benson, efficient as always, had followed Adam's progress along Dockside and the Rolls was parked right in front of the store. The chauffeur stepped forward and Katie handed over the bag of books without a quibble. The book-buying experience must end at the curb, Adam decided.

''I did. And some really interesting people.'' Her expression lit up like a floodlight as she cast a pleased glance around her. ''This is a charmingly provincial little town. I only wish I'd found it sooner.''

As Adam came up behind her, hoping to hurry her into the car and save some of what remained of the morning, she pressed her hands to the small of her back and bent backward in a supple stretch... bringing into pointed focus the fact that she had breasts. A rather nicely rounded set, too. He couldn't help but notice, and even though he'd been treated to the sight of thrust-out chests quite often, he realized no woman had ever been quite so unselfconscious about it.

He realized he was still staring when she uncurved her body and came upright again, a tiny furrow of concentration between her brows, the light of speculation in her very blue eyes. ''You know,'' she said, as if speaking to no one in particular. ''The way the light poles are made, it would be super easy to hang those decorative flags from them. The ones that have firecrackers for the Fourth of July and tulips for spring and snowmen for winter.'' Her gaze came back to him and she smiled. ''Maybe you should suggest that at your town meeting.''

''Too simple a solution for Sea Change,'' he said, wishing she'd just get in the car, but realizing in the next instant her suggestion had merit. Flags bearing symbols of the season might be a feasible alternative to the tinsel reindeer proposed by some and the jingle-bell wreaths supported by others. Flags. Simple, tasteful, and possible. Now how had she done that? He regarded her backside as she climbed into the Rolls. A rather nice backside, it was, too. And, despite the fact that her toenails were painted a startling shade of neon pink and one toe sported a slender silver band, the flash of ankles and slender calves couldn't help but catch his eye. Who was this woman, anyway? He was beginning to wonder if he should have hired her on Ilsa Fairchild's recommendation alone. On the other hand, there was no getting around the fact that she was creative. And different. And here, which meant he didn't have to waste any more time finding someone else to plan the party.

"Benson," he said. "Let's get out of town before we lose her again."

"Yes, sir." The chauffeur tugged the brim of his cap. "She did lead you quite a chase, didn't she, sir?" Benson had been chauffeuring the Braddock brothers from place to place for more than twenty years and was as much a part of the extended family as anyone else at the Hall. He never trespassed on the boundaries of the relationship, of course, but he didn't hesitate to share a little joke now and then, either.

"Yes," Adam said. "She did."

And he was all set to discuss that point with her, too, when he climbed into the car to take his seat beside her.

But she was talking on her cell phone and didn't seem to know he was there.

Chapter Three

Imagination was Katie's strong suit. She'd needed a good one growing up in a house where children were considered more trouble than they were worth. Her grandparents had been good people at heart, but if they'd ever known much happiness it had died with her father and there was simply none left over to give to her. Living with them, she'd had the basic food, clothing and shelter, but any joy she found in the lonely hours and minutes that made up her days, she had to create on her own. So she taught herself to anticipate every pleasure, savor the sights and sounds she could imagine every bit as much or more than the reality when it came. But as accomplished as her imagination was, Braddock Hall was nothing like she'd thought it would be.

From her first glimpse of the house through the smoky tint of the car window to the moment Adam had basically abandoned her in a foyer large enough to hold an orchestra, Katie had been almost afraid to blink for fear the house would vanish in a poof of unsettling reality. But in the hour she'd been strolling from room to room, unchallenged and undisturbed, the place had only improved, taken on a touchable, livable type of charm—if a home as elegant as this one and the size of a small hospital besides, could correctly be called charming.

She'd seen pictures of New England estates, of course, the huge multi-story dwellings that were rightly called the castles of America. She'd even caught glimpses of some of them when she'd lived a few months on Long Island. But she'd never actually seen one up close before and to be turned loose on her own reconnaissance... Well, her imagination was taking a back seat to reality today, that was for sure!

It would have been nice to have a guide on her excursion, someone to give her a bit of history on the house, but Adam had made it clear to her in the presence of a poker-faced butler named Abbott that he had pressing matters of business to attend, and she should wander the house and grounds at will. He'd instructed her to inform Abbott, who would, in turn, inform Benson, when she was ready to return to the city. Then he'd walked off, asking questions of Abbott as he went, dialing a number on the cell phone at the same time, his attention already tuned in to the problematic buyout, and oblivious to the considerable merits of her most appealing smile. He and the butler had disappeared behind a pair of heavy wooden doors before she could ask either one of them to point her in the general direction of the ladies' room.

But according to Rorie, who talked as if she knew, there wasn't much need for a ladies' room, this being strictly a household of men. No female had lived within the walls of Braddock Hall since Adam's grandmother had died two years before. There was a housekeeper, Ruth, but she lived in Sea Change, rode her bicycle back and forth on pleasant days, was picked up by Benson the rest of the time and, according to Rorie, wouldn't open her mouth to say hello to those who were dying to find out what went on behind the great walls of the estate.

Apparently the Braddocks were much talked about in the village of Sea Change. At least by the womenfolk there. Not that there was—also according to Rorie, who had proved to be a veritable fountain of gossip—much information forthcoming from those who worked on the estate, a closemouthed bunch, the lot of them, though it wasn't from lack of effort on the part of the townspeople. In addition to Ruth, there was a quartet of women from Providence who came Monday through Friday to clean and there were also a couple of female gardeners among the mostly male crew of groundskeepers, but by and large, Braddock Hall was an enclave of males. Adam's grandfather and Adam, along with his two younger brothers, Bryce and Peter, all resided at the Hall…more or less. The father, James, visited from time to time but almost never stayed more than a night or two. Usually, he brought his current wife—a position that changed, according to Rorie, as regularly as the season. But if other women ever spent the night at Braddock Hall, it wasn't reported to the local folks. The family was zealously protective of their privacy.

And so, the Brothers Braddock formed a mysterious fraternity, a hotbed of speculation, a source of endless fascination for the residents of the town, and they were the embodiment of every wish Rorie Reynolds had ever made on the evening star. That much Katie had figured out for herself within the first ten minutes of their chat.

But now that she was seeing the place firsthand, she could understand the level of interest. If she lived in Sea Change, she'd probably spend a disproportionate amount of time discussing the Braddock men, too. There was a great deal of history in the house, the synergy of power and traces of a family life. Hard to believe that Adam Braddock *had* a family life, but there were photographs all around declaring that he did. Katie looked at everything without compunction and tried to imagine the family that had created Adam, the automated businessman. She was tempted to open the doors he'd disappeared behind and ask him flat-out what it had been like to grow up in this wonderful house, but a set of open French doors and an expanse of greenery called her outside, instead.

This, she decided after a few soft breaths of fragrance, was where she would like to retire. Maybe Braddock Hall could use a female statue. She'd spent one week as a live mannequin in Marshall Field's Houston store. She could put the experience to good use here—just stand perfectly still in this beautiful flower garden and be decorative. Not that Adam would notice…unless she attached a cell phone to her hip. Katie sighed, wishing it didn't bother her so much to be ignored by him. It wasn't as if she wanted his attention. Well, okay, so she wouldn't mind a little flirtation, a yin and yang kind of conversational exchange. He was a very attractive man and it was only human to want to believe he found her at least somewhat attractive, too. But then, inevitably, he'd want to know what she had planned for his grandfather's party and she'd have to explain that she was not a party planner. Never had been. And from there...well, things could not come to a good end.

A low, tuneful whistling of "Baby, Let Your Hair Hang Low" drew her around a maze of shrubbery to a hothouse formed of frosted glass panels. An elderly man in bright blue coveralls was just inside the open doorway, mixing potting soil and enjoying his work, if the whistling was a good indication. "Hi," she said softly, not wanting to startle him by her sudden presence.

He looked up, and his green eyes took in her appearance in a spry glance. Then, he straightened and dusted his gloved hands against his coveralls. "Well, hello," he said. "Who might you be?"

"I might be a water sprite in search of a lily pond or a butterfly looking for a garden," she answered blithely catching a glimpse of the extensive flowerings inside the greenhouse. "But I'm actually just a pseudo party planner who was told to tour the grounds, so that's what I'm doing. And thoroughly enjoying it, too."

"Told by whom?" The gardener inquired.

"Adam." She thought she recognized a fragrant waxy bloom and couldn't believe it would prosper so far from its tropical habitat. "Is that a plumeria?"

He glanced behind him and nodded. "Fragile, but doing its best to give me the blooms I'm after. You say *Adam* told you to look around?"

"Yes. Adam Braddock. The owner." She

frowned. "Or one of them, at any rate. Do you know him?"

The old man smiled. "Oh, yes. I know him."

"Well, of course. I didn't mean you wouldn't. I'm sure he's a very, uh, *hands-on* employer."

His laugh was aged with life and mellow, like a good wine. "I don't think I'd go so far as to say that."

She laughed, too, glad they had a basic understanding already. "He thinks I'm an events planner," she said confidingly. "He wouldn't believe me when I said he'd dialed the wrong number and he wouldn't take no for an answer, so here I am, roaming the place at will. You'd think he'd be a little more careful." She realized how that might sound. "Not that I'm a threat to anybody. But he really should pay more attention to what people are trying to say to him."

"He has a great deal on his mind and doesn't always listen as well as he ought to, that's true." The old man reached beside the door frame, picked up a polished-wood cane to aid in balancing as he stepped over the threshold and out of the greenhouse. "So he dialed your phone number by mistake and that's how you wound up here today?"

She felt a little embarrassed at her runaway tongue, but she'd always had a knack for recognizing a kindred spirit, and besides, it was a bit late for scruples now. "Actually, he thinks that a mutual friend gave him my number…and well, she probably did. But it had to be by accident, not design. I mean, no one who knows me would ever mistake me for an events planner."

His smile widened at that. "This mutual friend...may I ask her name?"

It was an odd question for him to ask, but there seemed no good reason not to tell him. "Ilsa Fairchild."

"Ilsa," he said, his voice softening with pleasure. "Then you must be...?"

"Katie," she said, extending her hand. "Katie Canton."

"Katie," he repeated with a soft, slow regard, as if her name, itself, pleased him in some intangible way. He braced his weight with the cane as he stripped off one of the dirty canvas gloves and grasped her outstretched hand. "Archer Braddock," he said.

Katie's grip faltered. "B-Braddock? You're one of...?"

"The family, but I hope you won't hold that against me." His eyes twinkled with delight at her chagrin. "As it happens, I'm the best listener of the bunch...even though I can be quite deaf when it suits me."

She laughed in spite of her embarrassment...or perhaps because of it. "I'm sorry if I—"

"Don't give it a second thought. You didn't say anything I wouldn't say myself. My grandsons don't listen to me either, if that's any consolation to you. And Adam's the worst of the lot. He never listens when he ought to, or maybe I should say, *especially* when he ought to." He tossed the gloves on top of the mound of potting soil. "So, Katie, let's talk about you, but first, please tell me you'll be staying for dinner."

"Oh, I don't think my invitation runs that long."
She fell into a slow, but steady walk beside him.
"I'm to let Abbott know so he can let Benson know
as soon as I'm ready to return to Providence."

"Surely my grandson offered you some lunch?"

"No," she said, realizing she was hungry. "I'm
sure it never crossed his mind. He's a very busy guy,
as I'm sure you've noticed."

Archer Braddock shook his head. "I worry about
that boy, but never mind, my dear, you'll have lunch
with me. Then Adam can take you out for dinner this
evening when you both get back into Providence."

"I don't think that's very likely," she said. "I
accused him of being a closet eater on the way down
here and he didn't deny it."

Archer looked startled, then he laughed. "And my
grandson didn't take the hint and invite you out for
dinner?"

"Oh, it wasn't a hint," Katie said, wanting to ensure this nice man didn't think she was making a
play for his grandson. According to Rorie, every
woman who met Adam Braddock fell panting at his
feet and, if that were true, Katie wanted to be sure
to abstain. "Just an observation."

"And an astute one at that." He nodded toward
the house. "It's such a lovely day, would you enjoy
having lunch on the terrace?"

"Looking out on these wonderful gardens? I'd like
that more than anything," she said and meant it.

ADAM HEARD the laughter all the way in his office.
It drifted across his conversation with Lara as a dim
distraction and then settled vaguely, but pleasingly

into his consciousness. Eventually, the sound and a persistent empty sensation in his stomach drew him out to the terrace, where his grandfather and Katie were looking relaxed and happy, seated at a table which bore the traces of a leisurely lunch.

"I see you two have met," he said, pulling out a chair and thinking the gardens looked especially nice this year. Katie looked especially nice, too, the red of her blouse making a nice spot of color against the lush green backdrop of the gardens, her cheeks flushed, her eyes sparkling, a rather fascinating trace of laughter lingering in her smile. He had another fleeting sense of recognition, a déjà vu wisp of knowing, but couldn't place it before it slipped away. "Got the party plans all worked out?"

"We've been talking about Shakespeare," Archer said. "And salmonella."

Adam raised his eyebrows. "Neither, I hope, are on the invitation list."

"Believe it or not," Katie said, "the party hasn't been mentioned."

"Except in the beginning," Archer pointed out with the alacrity of easy friendship. "When you were explaining how you came to be wandering alone in my gardens."

"Oh, yes, except for then." She smiled at him and he smiled back, as if they shared a delicious secret. Her big blue eyes shifted reluctantly, it seemed, to Adam. "Did you get the company?"

He frowned. "Company? Oh, you mean the Wallace Company. Not yet. The deal is still cooking, but things are looking less grim than they were this morning, thanks to your suggestion."

"You made a suggestion?" Archer asked her, as if she'd done a very brave thing indeed. "To my grandson?"

She shrugged. "It was just a thought."

Archer raised a trim white eyebrow at Adam, although his words were addressed to Katie. "And he took it?"

Adam reined in a twinge of impatience. He didn't mind giving Katie credit for her insight, but he didn't think his grandfather should make it sound as if just considering her idea was some sort of once-in-a-lifetime honor. "Katie overheard a conversation I was having with Lara and suggested Wallace might be concerned about his employees. The idea seemed plausible to me. It's a family business, you know. He promotes it that way. We'd made some provisions for the transition period, of course, but recompense for his employees wasn't specifically addressed when we put together the original deal."

"And you're considering compensating the employees? Isn't that going to make the buyout prohibitively expensive?"

"It'll cost us less in the long run, as we hope most of the employees from middle management levels down will stay with us."

Archer nodded approvingly. "So this little lady saved your bacon."

Adam wouldn't have put it quite like that. "She had a good thought on the matter," he said, hearing how stiff and priggish the admission sounded. "It remains to be seen whether that will solve Wallace's problem with the deal, although Lara believes that only a slight compromise from us will have a good effect on the deliberations.''

"Good thinking," Archer said, but he addressed Katie, bestowing on her a goodly share of genteel charm. "Where did you learn about company take-overs?"

"You've just heard pretty much all I know on the subject.'' She ran her fingers through her dark hair and Adam noted the way the curls bounced and shone in the aftermath. She wasn't beautiful, but there was something quite striking about the ivory sheen of her skin set off by the rich, nearly black luster of her hair, and the Hawaiian-blue of her eyes. Or maybe it was the thick smudge of dark lashes that set off those eyes. Or maybe it was the bright red of her shirt. Or maybe he was just out of his head with hunger. Leaning forward, he pulled a leftover grape from its stem and popped it into his mouth. "You're being falsely modest, Katie. You said you used to work in a brokerage house.''

She tipped her head to the side, the furrow of a frown edging onto her forehead. "It was only for about six months, just long enough to pick up the gossip around the water cooler.''

"You have insight into what makes people tick and that kind of understanding can't be taught in business school," Archer said, a glimmer of interest in his eyes that hadn't been seen there in quite a long time. "Too few people have it these days, as it is.''

"Thank you, Mr. Braddock, but I really can't take too much credit. I'm sure Adam and his corporate team would have secured the Wallace Company without my, very, offhand observation.''

"Correct," Adam said. "We certainly would have. But it's possible your idea has speeded the process along."

"So what kind of reward are you giving her?" Archer wanted to know.

Adam frowned meaningfully at his grandfather. "My thanks, possibly yours."

"You should take her out to dinner, Adam. To show your appreciation."

Adam caught the subtle *What-do-you-say-to-that?* arching of her brow. "A delightful idea, Grandfather, but the thing is, I don't eat dinner."

Her lips curved with sudden—and surprised— pleasure at his response and something went wrong with his pulse. It raced, jumped track and filled his head with totally inappropriate thoughts. He made a show of glancing at his watch, suddenly anxious to escape before he said something he'd regret like, *Why don't we have dinner together?* "I've got to go into town for the council meeting," he said instead. "Please excuse me. Grandfather." He nodded to Archer, smiled noncommittally at Katie. "Whenever you're ready to leave—"

"Tell Abbott to tell Benson. I remember."

"I thought you were returning to Providence tonight, too, Adam," Archer said.

"I am, but I practically kidnapped Katie today. You know how unpredictable these meetings can be and I don't want her to waste her entire afternoon waiting on me."

"I don't mind," Katie said, shooting his escape in the foot. "I'm having a wonderful time and—" she

paused, looked down, then met his gaze again
"—I'd really like to talk to you before I leave."

"Good, she'll wait for you." Archer declared, settling the issue with a heavy hand. "I'll show her
around. Give her the twenty-five-cent grand tour.
Tell her more than she could ever want to know
about the family history. And if we run out of interesting topics of conversation, maybe we'll talk about
my birthday party."

"Excellent," Adam said, because there was never
any point in arguing with Archer. "Lord only knows
when this meeting will end, but I'll hurry it as best
I can." He stood, wishing he could just stay on the
terrace and watch the flowers grow or perhaps, just
watch Katie. "I may suggest your flag idea, Katie,
and see if that speeds things along."

"Flag idea?" Archer asked, looking at Katie with
a question.

"It was nothing," she said. "Just a thought that
decorative, seasonal flags would look really nice
hanging from those wonderful, old-fashioned street-
light poles."

Archer laughed aloud, a sound too often missing
in the two years since Grandmother had died and one
Adam was only too happy to hear again...even if it
came at his expense. "Old-fashioned? Do you hear
that, Adam? She thinks your newfangled streetlights
are old-fashioned." He leaned confidingly closer to
Katie. "He convinced the town council to put in
those lights last year. Funny thing is, they look exactly like the ones they replaced."

"They are, however, energy-efficient and safe,

now," Adam pointed out. "I still think I pulled off a major coup when I got that past the council."

"I can't imagine anyone in town would ever argue with you," Katie said.

"Hard to imagine, perhaps, but true," he replied, intrigued by the subtle flash of a dimple in her cheek. "The people on the council keep me humble."

"I'm sure they have to work very hard at it."

She smiled a smile that could launch a thousand ships and Adam caught his breath, deciding he needed to get going now, rather than later. "You and Katie work out the arrangements for your party, Grandfather, and I'll be home as quickly as town attitude allows. Sooner, if a miracle occurs."

"Maybe it already has," Archer said. "You know, now that I've met Katie and discovered how imaginative and creative she is, I'm beginning to look forward to my birthday party with great anticipation."

"So am I," Adam said, realizing as he turned to walk away that it was true.

Unsettlingly, undeniably true.

A DOOR SLAMMED with a far-off, muffled thud and several minutes later, Katie heard quick, no-nonsense footsteps in the hallway. She looked up from the book she was reading in time to see a young man with windblown blond hair stride purposefully past the open library doors. "Hi, Ruth," he called as he passed. A moment slipped by before he skidded back to the doorway to take another look. "Whoa, Ruth," he said. "You've slimmed down since yesterday. Changed your hair color, too."

"Grapefruit diet," Katie said with a grin as she

tousled her new hairdo. "And a trip to the beauty salon."

He grinned, too. "Whatever you paid, it was worth it and then some. You look fantastic." He came into the library where she'd been investigating a bit of Rhode Island history and extended a friendly hand. "Hello, I'm Bryce and, unless you're in a really great disguise, you're not our housekeeper."

"I'm Katie Canton," she said, returning his handshake.

He stepped back and regarded her with frank admiration. "You're not by any chance the new upstairs maid, are you?"

"Not the downstairs maid, either." So this was Adam's brother, Bryce. The resemblance was unmistakable. The men shared similar facial features and the same strong bone structure still visible in Archer's wrinkled face. Only in Bryce there was less intensity, a more easygoing, what-you-see-is-what-you-get, openness than in either his grandfather or his older brother. He had blond hair, blue eyes, was perhaps slightly shorter, but overall more athletic in appearance than Adam. Where Adam seemed cool and reserved, Bryce was all warmth and devilish charm. Katie had met men like him before and knew it was best to take the flirtation they offered like a breath mint, enjoyable for short bursts of flavor, but not something one should depend on for the long haul. "I'm just here for the twenty-five-cent tour, which lasted almost an hour and a half and ended about," she glanced at her serviceable Seiko wrist watch, "forty-five minutes ago. Your grandfather had to stop for his afternoon lie-down."

"Hard to believe any Braddock worth his salt would take a nap with you in the house, but Grandfather has to have his lie-downs. Can I get you a lemonade? Water? Soda? Champagne? Caviar?"

"No, thanks. I expect Adam will be back any time and then we'll be returning to Providence."

Bryce waved the information aside as if it were a pesky mosquito. "Forget Adam. I'll take you anywhere you want to go. Fresno, Santa Fe, Amsterdam?"

She laughed. "I've already been to the first two and Amsterdam is still pretty far down the list. Baton Rouge is actually next on my agenda."

"No, no, no," he said, flirting all the more persistently. "You do not want to visit Louisiana in the summer. Trust me on this, Katie Canton. I would never lie to you about heat and humidity. Everything else, well, I might be tempted to stretch the truth on other topics, but weather? No, I'll always be straight with you about that." He smiled easily and sank into the chair opposite her, leaning forward, his attention all for her. "Are you staying for dinner?"

"I've already stayed through lunch."

"Doesn't matter. Dinner will be better with me here to entertain you. I was only stopping by to pick up something, but I'll stay if you'll stay. I'm nothing if not flexible when the situation involves a beautiful woman."

She imagined that was most certainly true. "I'm afraid it's up to Adam to decide whether or not we stay for dinner, but thanks for offering to change your plans for me. It's not necessary."

"Necessity is in the eye of the beholder," he said.

"And I will be greatly beholden to you if you'll ditch my unimaginative big brother for me. He won't have noticed how beautiful you are because of all those stock quotes rolling across his corneas from morning to night. I can see by the look on your face that you've noticed his vacant and bemused stare."

"Disparaging me behind my back, Bryce?" Adam asked from the doorway. "That's unworthy of you."

Bryce greeted his brother with a cocky smile. "Just holding your place for you, big brother."

Adam walked into the library as quietly as he'd approached the doorway. If he'd been a mouse, he'd have had her cheese and gone before she'd known he was in the room. "Have you had a pleasant afternoon, Katie?" he asked. "I'm sorry the meeting lasted as long as it did, but you'll be happy to know your flag idea has been taken under consideration and the mayor appointed a committee to research the possibilities. I don't hold out a lot of hope, but your suggestion met with less initial opposition than the tinsel reindeer or the jingle bell wreaths, which are also being considered."

"Is that why you're here and not in the office keeping our family fortunes compounding?" Bryce asked, looking rather unconvincingly offended. "Christmas decorations? And just Saturday you canceled our handball game because you were too busy to get away from the office for an hour. Admit it, Adam, you were just afraid I'd whip your ass...ets into shape on the court." He covered nicely and treated Katie to a saintly smile. "I beat him regularly at handball."

"Only because I have all those stock quotes scroll-

ing in front of my eyes all the while I'm playing,''
Adam said, stopping behind an elegant little wooden
chair and resting his arms along the curve of the
back, leaning into the triangle of their conversation,
looking casually intrigued and quite remarkably attractive. "And I'm here because as chairman of the
town council, it is my responsibility to be at the
meetings.''

"Oh, well, if we're talking about responsibility, I
completely understand.'' Bryce waved a hand dis-
missively. "Nothing should interfere with the high
calling of responsibility.''

The tension was palpable for a moment. Katie felt
it like a morning fog, thick and disorienting, but then
as quickly as it came, it was gone in the sunny flash
of Bryce's smile. "Personally, I was just taking the
responsibility of persuading Katie that dinner at the
Hall is mandatory, now that I'm home.''

"I thought you were crewing for Holden Locke
this week,'' Adam said.

"I am.'' Bryce continued to court Katie with his
eyes. "I'm due in Newport to hook up with the rest
of the *Andrea Cara* crew about six.''

"Doesn't that preclude having dinner here?''

"Don't sweat it, Adam. Holden won't sail without
me.''

Adam's jaw tightened. Katie watched the muscle
flex with his tension and decided he was biting his
tongue to keep the family peace. But whether for her
benefit or his own, she couldn't tell. "Did Grandfather show you all you wanted to see?'' he asked her.
"Any problems present themselves?''

"Problems?''

"About the setup for the party."

"The party?" Bryce asked.

Adam glanced at his brother. "Katie is the events coordinator I've hired to plan Grandfather's birthday celebration. That's why she's here."

Bryce's frown chastised her. "And I thought you'd wrangled an invitation from Adam just to meet me."

While it was flattering to be the object of Bryce Braddock's attention, Katie had a sneaky suspicion that Grandma Moses would have gotten the same treatment had she been the only available woman when these two brothers were in the same room. There was competition here and a lack of understanding between the two men. Katie could see it, feel it and right or wrong, she thought the major fault was Adam's. "If I were that clever, I'd have already figured out where I'd be having dinner."

Bryce's smile was quick and triumphant. "Good, it's settled, you're staying."

"Great." Adam curved his hands over the chair back as he straightened. "I'm hungry. I'll let Abbott know there'll be four of us for dinner." He turned, then glanced back. "I don't suppose Peter will surprise us by coming home tonight."

"I spoke to him this morning," Bryce said, standing. "He's staying in Atlanta until Thursday, but he'll be here this weekend. Since we've got an hour or so before dinner, mind if I take Katie for a quick spin in the Ferrari?"

Adam's jaw worked again, but his smile was pleasant enough. "That's something you'll need to ask her. As far as I know, she's a free agent."

Katie felt like she'd just been handed over, from brother to brother, à la carte. "I've never ridden in a Ferrari before," she said. "On the other hand, I'd never ridden in a Rolls-Royce before today, either." She shot Adam a challenging glance. "What an adventure for me, huh?"

"He drives too fast," was Adam's only comment.

"He doesn't drive much at all," was Bryce's reply.

"It would be difficult to drive and conduct business at the same time," Katie said neutrally. No way was she putting herself between these two powerful personalities. "I'd love to take that drive, Bryce. If you're sure you don't mind, Adam?"

The flicker in his gaze told her he did mind, but wouldn't dream of admitting it. "Why would I? If you're satisfied with your tour of the house and grounds, I certainly have no reason to object."

Which meant, probably, that he did have reason. But this wasn't her battle and Katie figured if she had to stay for dinner—and it looked like she did—then she might as well add *ride in a Ferrari* to her list of the day's adventures. "Great," she said and smiled at Bryce as she laid the history book aside and rose to her feet with an eager bounce. "Can I drive?"

Chapter Four

There was something familiar about the way Katie laughed. Adam knew he must have met her somewhere before, but the time and place and circumstances eluded him. Or maybe her lovely laugh only seemed familiar because he'd heard it so often during dinner that it seemed he must have known it all his life. Bryce had outdone himself at being charming, and Grandfather had been no slouch in that department either. If entertaining Katie was the goal, the Braddock men had certainly risen to the challenge. Except for Adam, who had mainly watched her laugh at things he hadn't had the ease or opportunity to say.

Growing up, Adam had often felt the weight of his birthright sitting squarely on his shoulders. There had been times, although not many, when he'd envied his younger brothers their ability to have fun as they pleased, without having to worry about the duties and responsibilities he, as the oldest, had inherited. He'd had to be serious, studious and committed, because, in his heart, he felt that was his designated role in the family. He would be the man his father wasn't and, thereby, make his grandparents proud. But to-night, for whatever reason, Adam wished he could feel the freedom Bryce felt to charm Katie Canton and make her laugh.

For some reason, the whole evening had put him on edge. Perhaps it was as simple as the fact that he'd wanted to get back to Providence immediately after the town meeting. Or as complicated as the way Bryce had manipulated Katie into staying for dinner. Or maybe it was just because Adam felt responsible for bringing her here and exposing her to his brother's blatant flirtation, although in general, it was his belief that women who sat at this dinner table should be perfectly capable of handling a little light flirtation.

Katie certainly seemed capable of giving as good as she got. She was quite skilled in the art, too, en-chanting both Bryce and Grandfather in the process. Okay, so Adam had to admit he was charmed, as well. It wasn't just the laugh, or the sparkle of mis-chief in her dancing blue eyes, although those cer-tainly added to her attractions. It was more a com-bination of the whole Katie package and, though he would never say so, there were moments during the evening when he thought he might be happy for days just watching the variations of her smile.

At other moments during the evening, when his brother was putting forth extra effort to charm her, Adam told himself he was only concerned that Katie shouldn't read more into the attention than it merited. Bryce charmed a dozen women a day, maybe more. He flirted the same way he did everything else—with boundless enthusiasm. And he broke at least one heart a week, just to keep in practice.

That wasn't entirely fair. Bryce broke hearts, true, but not that often and certainly never with any malicious intent. He did it as unconsciously as he breathed and was honestly amazed to learn someone had taken his flirting seriously. On occasion, afterward, he even tried mightily to set things to right. Adam had told him for years that if he'd behave more responsibly in the first place, nothing would *need* to be set aright. But while Bryce was often, in Adam's admittedly biased opinion, careless with other's emotions, he was, at heart, a kind and decent young man whose major flaw was anchored in his greatest attribute—his extraordinary gift for living life full out and without limits.

But whether his brother was hero or cad, Adam didn't want him toying with Katie. He wanted her to concentrate on the upcoming birthday party and he wanted Bryce to let her do it in peace. Or maybe he only wanted not to see her laugh so spiritedly at Bryce's every comment.

Dinner passed with conversation ranging from the frivolous to the absurd, never once—despite Adam's occasional efforts—settling into the discussion he had hoped to generate about the upcoming birthday party. Instead, his questions prompted a reminiscence of great parties of the past. Archer took the lead in relating anecdotes from parties past, happily spilling out humorous moments in the Braddock family history like a string of pearls, all apparently told with one purpose in mind—to hear Katie laugh.

By the time dinner was over and Bryce suggested

he drive Katie home, even Adam had been lulled into a pleasantly congenial good humor. His brother's suggestion snapped him back to reality with an unsettling jolt of alarm. For all her considerable skill at flirting, Katie was largely unsophisticated and therefore, in his opinion, ill-equipped to handle Bryce's charm after dark. Adam knew it was none of his business, but he'd brought Katie, rather insistently, to his home today, introduced her, however unintentionally, to his brother, and he felt it was therefore his responsibility to see that she got home safely. All that was needed to turn the upcoming birthday party into a disaster was for her to think Bryce meant even half of the flowery compliments he handed out so effortlessly.

"Providence is out of your way," he said, intervening smoothly. "I'll see that Katie gets home safely."

"I believe she'd prefer to go with me," Bryce replied just as smoothly, with an *of-course-you-would* wink at her.

"Nonetheless, I'll take her home." Adam was in no mood to argue about this.

"I don't think so," Bryce said, ready to rumble.

"Katie," Archer said. "While I'd love to insist that these young men allow *me* to escort you back to Providence, I'm afraid old age conquers chivalry this time around. You'll just have to make do with one of my grandsons."

Katie's smile was soft with appreciation. "It is, truly, the thought that counts, Mr. Braddock."

"Then you'll ride with me," Bryce said.

"No," Adam stated, brooking no further disagreement.

"I'm extremely flattered to have *two* Braddock brothers intent on seeing me home," she said easily. "But I think I'll just try my thumb at hitchhiking back. I've already ridden in a Rolls-Royce and a Ferrari today, and it may not be too late to see if I can catch a lift in a Lamborghini."

Bryce laughed as if she'd made a great joke. Even Archer smiled at the ridiculous idea. But Adam didn't see anything funny in the image of Katie on a dark road—or a well-lighted one, for that matter—using her thumb...or worse, her well-turned ankle to flag down a stranger. What sort of life had she led to think the idea romantic even in jest? She talked as if she were savvy and streetwise, but there was a vulnerability in her expression she tried to hide, the occasional shadow in her pretty eyes. It must be the contradiction he found so interesting, he decided. Either that, or he was still under the spell of her laughter.

"You'll go with me," he said, determined to protect her for the thirty or forty minutes it would take to return to Providence. "I believe you had something you wanted to discuss with me?"

Her smile paled, but immediately brightened again. "I did say that this afternoon, didn't I? How...effective...of you to remember."

It took several goodbyes and an equal number of invitations to return to the Hall, before Benson finally closed the door of the Rolls behind them and drove past the sturdy old stone wall that bordered the estate. Alone with Katie, Adam felt an obligation to show that he could be as conversant as his brother, despite the lack of evidence during dinner. "My brother must have taken you on quite a spin before dinner. You were gone an hour and fifteen minutes." Not exactly the sparkling wit he'd hoped to display. Not subtle, either, but a subject he felt needed to be addressed. "Did you enjoy your ride in his Ferrari?"

Katie's gaze swivelled to him. "An expensive sports car and an attractive, attentive young man? What woman wouldn't enjoy that kind of ride?"

"He didn't, uh, drive too fast for you?"

"He didn't, as a matter of fact. I, on the other hand, may have scared his pants off when I opened that baby up."

"He let you drive?" Fast on the heels of that question, another thought struck him. "You said you don't drive."

Her eyebrows arched. "I don't. That doesn't mean I don't know how, only that the opportunity doesn't come along very often."

"Do you have a license?" Dumb and irrelevant, and not at all what he really wanted to know.

"To drive? Or to scare the pants off your brother?"

She was a mile ahead of him, Adam realized so he moved straight to the point. "Katie, you may be the only woman Bryce has taken for a drive in his Ferrari…today. Then again, you may be the sixteenth or twentieth."

"Mmm," she said on a dramatic sigh. "And I was so certain he fell madly and irrevocably in love with me the very moment our eyes met."

"I thought you should be aware, that's all."

Her smile bounced back, bearing a tinge of apology for teasing him. "I do appreciate the warning, Adam, but it's totally unnecessary. I've been taking care of myself for so long, I can spot trouble way down the road and, when I see it coming, I always cross the street. You don't have to worry that I took your brother seriously because I didn't."

Adam was relieved. Absurdly so. "Good."

"I'm sure he'd be horrified if he thought I had."

"Yes, I expect he would."

"Oh, admit it, Adam, you'd be horrified, too." Her smile unsettled him all the more. "If I were to start chasing after your brother, I'd be bound to neglect the birthday party and that could cause you all kinds of problems."

True, absolutely. But he could spot trouble, too, even if he didn't always choose to cross the street when he saw it coming. "On the contrary, I'm convinced you're a consummate professional, Katie. I doubt a hurricane would distract you once you started on a project."

"Oh, a hurricane would do it. I'm not good in storms." Her gaze cut to him, then quickly away and she plucked nervously at a loose string on her dress. "But since we're talking about the party, sort of, there is, uh, something I need to tell you."

Now that she'd seen the house and grounds—and driven the Ferrari—she wanted more money. He could feel a renegotiation coming, and was surprised at the level of his disappointment. "Yes?"

The string plucking intensified. "I tried to tell you this before," she began. "I can't..." Her voice trailed away, then came back with a sharp inhale.

"I'm not the person you need for this. I'm just not…right for the job."

"You want more money to do it," he said, cutting to the chase.

"No." She couldn't have sounded more definite, nor looked more amazed. "Good grief, no. Are you kidding? I couldn't begin to earn the amount of money already on the table. What I meant was just what I said. I'm not—repeat, *not*—the right person for the job."

She didn't want to up the ante. He could hardly believe it, but for some reason, he did, and the relief was so strong, he nearly laughed aloud. "On the contrary, Katie, you're the perfect person. After the way you charmed my grandfather today, I wouldn't dare bring anyone else in to plan his party."

"But you're making a mistake," she said and started to go on, but he stopped her, realizing now that all the talk about past parties must have worried her.

"Don't let the size of the house and grounds intimidate you, Katie. I'm sure you have enough experience with caterers and florists, and the like, to plan a delightful evening. But even if you didn't, I'd much prefer to have someone with your enthusiasm and originality than someone with thousands of successful events under her belt."

"How about someone with a couple of complete disasters under her belt?"

He wanted to reach over and take her hand, reassure her with a touch, but that, of course, would be inappropriate. "We all learn by making mistakes. And at the risk of sounding arrogant, Braddock parties are always successful. There just isn't much you can do to ruin one. In any case, if I'm not worried about your qualifications, I don't see why you should be."

She looked at him with frank curiosity. "Is there anything you *do* worry about, Adam?"

"I either take action on a problem or put it aside until I can make a decision about how to deal with it. Worry simply isn't in my vocabulary."

"Now, *that* sounded arrogant."

He laughed. "Okay, so maybe I'm somewhat acquainted with the concept. But that doesn't solve your problem. Tell me what really worries you, Katie."

She sighed and her gaze turned to the moonlit landscape beyond the window and yet another of New England's sturdy old stone fences. "Stone walls," she said. "I'm worried that someday I'm going to run into one I can't get past."

"From what I observed tonight, you could probably persuade one to crumble with just a smile."

"I may have to give that a try, since talking apparently isn't going to do it."

"If you're worried about this party measuring up to past parties, I wish you wouldn't. I said in the beginning that you'd have carte blanche and I meant it. The budget, while not unlimited, is certainly generous. It is Grandfather's seventy-ninth birthday and my brothers and I aren't going to argue over the expense."

"Really. It seemed to me that you and Bryce have the art of argument down pat."

"Appearances are often deceiving." The stiffness

returned to his voice in a landslide. "You shouldn't base your opinion of me or my brother on a single evening."

"I'm much more tolerant than that, Adam. I couldn't help noticing the rivalry, but you're right, it was only a few hours and it was tactless to mention it at all. Sorry if I brought up a touchy subject."

So much for thinking his stilted tones might have gone undetected. "Bryce and I have our differences, of course. But we are brothers and our family is very important to us."

"I never doubted it for a second." Her smile bloomed, gentling any possible offense. "I'm sure it can't be easy for him, always comparing himself to you."

Her observation startled him. "I can't imagine either of my brothers waste their time and energy on such a meaningless comparison."

"No, of course, you can't." She winced. "Ooh, that sounded not at all like what I meant to say, which was only that you have to be a really tough act to follow."

Her comment made him uncomfortable all over again, as if she had read a subtext in the evening that he had failed to see. Definitely time to shift the focus of the conversation to her. "And where did you learn so much about family dynamics, Katie? Your accent is definitely not New England."

"I've lived a lot of places, so the inflections are a hit-and-miss combination of everywhere and nowhere."

"A lot of places," he repeated, curious at her vagueness. "Give me a rundown."

She waved her hand, dismissing the information as of no real importance. "Seattle, San Jose, Topeka, Toledo, Cincinnati, Cheyenne, and that's only a few. I like to experience the feel of a place, get an idea of what it's like to live there." A rueful breath escaped her. "I guess I'm afraid if I stay too long in any one spot, I'll get bored."

He smiled at her obvious exaggeration. He couldn't imagine she would ever allow herself to be bored. There was just too much energy emanating from inside her. "What about your education? You must have stayed in one spot long enough to acquire a diploma."

She shrugged. "I've spent a few hours in the ivory halls of higher education, but I always come back to the belief that it's more important to collect knowledge than a piece of paper. So wherever I find myself, I just take classes that interest me and I volunteer a lot."

She consistently managed to surprise him. "What kind of volunteer work?"

"You name it and I've probably done it at one time or another. The past few months, I've been doing some clerical work for the literacy program at the Providence Library."

"My grandmother was on the library board for years and the Braddock family is a big supporter of the library and the literacy effort."

"One of my favorite causes, too."

"Witnessed by your *weighty* passion for books."

"I admit it. I'm addicted to books of all shapes and sizes."

He was beginning to see how a man might become

addicted to her smile. It all but lit up the back of the Rolls. "It's nice to see someone whose enthusiasm for reading carries over into volunteering for a good cause."

"Hmm," she said, eyeing him with good humor. "Let me guess...you write the check and consider it a work well done."

"Wrong," he said. "I *sign* the check, after my secretary writes it out."

Her laugh was worth his denigrating stab at a joke. "You're teasing me," she said.

"Yes," he agreed, pleased to know he could. "My grandmother insisted on a tithe of time for all three of her grandsons. By the time I was nine, I was a seasoned volunteer. As a matter of fact..." He didn't mean to talk at length about the causes he supported with a whole heart, but she kept asking questions and her genuine interest created a reciprocal spark and he kept talking. When Benson stopped the Rolls in a modest suburban neighborhood, Adam realized he'd monopolized the conversation. He'd meant to know more about her at this juncture, had intended to be the one asking all the questions. Now how, he wondered, had she managed to keep the spotlight off herself?

"Here I am," she said, glancing over her shoulder at the house. "Benson certainly follows directions well, doesn't he? Well, good night, Adam. Thanks for a lovely day and—"

"I'll see you safely to your door," Adam said, strangely reluctant for the evening to end.

"Oh, no need to bother," she replied airily.

"There's no reason even for you to get out. I can see myself as far as the door, thanks."

She seemed to be in an unflattering hurry. "I'm getting out," he said, brooking no argument. "You've seen my house, now I'd like to see yours." It was either that or he had to say good night, something he was not yet ready to do.

She sighed, slid across the seat and stepped out, thanking Benson for his courtesy with a smile and insisting that she could carry the bag of books herself. At least, Adam thought, it wasn't just his help she objected to. He got out on the other side and was waiting when she walked around the rear of the Rolls-Royce. "Please," he said and took the bag of books from her arms. It was heavy, but he felt lighter just because she allowed him to carry it for her without a protest. Falling into step beside her, he walked up the sidewalk toward a house that seemed moderately upscale. It wasn't the Hall, of course, or even in the neighborhood, but as houses went, it was neat and nice, although not at all the kind of house he'd imagined Katie would like.

"It's not my house," she said, as if reading his thoughts. "I'm only sitting it while the owners are away."

Surprising. "I see," was the only comment he could think to make.

"I'm something of a professional housesitter, I guess you could say. That's one way I'm able to travel so much."

"There must be someplace you consider home."

"Home is where the heart is, as they say, so I'm pretty much home wherever I am."

That was a nifty bit of verbal footwork, but Adam knew there had to be more to her story. Before the birthday party, he decided, he'd discover what it was. "You have an interesting attitude for someone so young, Katie."

Her smile dimmed, but didn't go out. "I haven't been young since I was six years old." Stepping ahead of him, she unlocked the door and pushed it open. "Thanks," she said and he heard the rush of her breath, the sweet anxiety in her voice.

"You're welcome," he answered as he set the books inside. When he straightened to face her, the air was thick with a tension he recognized, an awareness he'd been trying to ignore all day, with little success. "Katie," he began, not sure what he wanted to say. "I'm glad Ilsa Fairchild gave me your name and number."

She bit her lip, brushed restlessly at her mop of dark curls, a gesture born of the awareness and tenderly compelling in its unselfconscious appeal. "Look, Adam, you have to listen to me for a minute. Really listen. I can't let you leave thinking I'm—"

Adam seldom acted on impulse, but he bent his head and pressed a very impulsive, claiming kiss to Katie's parted lips, interrupting her in midsentence and surprising her only slightly less than he'd surprised himself. She recovered more quickly than he did and then, even more surprisingly, returned his kiss with a gratifying enthusiasm. She seemed, in fact, to savor the feel of his lips on hers, the tantalizing brush of her body against his, the undeniable evidence that he found her desirable.

Her hands flattened slowly against his chest, then

moved to his shoulders where her fingers worked a restless massage through the weight of his suit coat. He wanted to take the coat off, but that would mean releasing her, something his arms—now that they had found their way around her—were reluctant to do. His hands slid to her waist and pulled her, pressed her closer to him in an embrace that turned passionate before he even knew that was his body's intent. When the kiss broke, he realized he could barely breathe and noted with an embarrassingly male satisfaction that she looked as dazed as he felt.

"Wow." Her whispered judgment seconded his own and he reached for her again, but she held him off with a firm hand pressed against the buttoned placket of his shirt. "It's not that I wouldn't enjoy doing that again, you understand, but one too many of those could dangerously overload my risk quota for today." She drew in a long, shaky breath. "A good-night kiss was not at all how I expected tonight to end."

"Believe it or not, I'm a little surprised, myself."

Her lips curved with a wry, self-effacing humor. "Oh, I believe you."

"I realize it's a breach of your strictly-professional policy, but I can't bring myself to apologize for something I enjoyed so much."

She took hold of the doorknob, as if she needed its support. "Well, you don't have to worry about that strictly professional thing anymore because...because I won't be planning your grandfather's party. I'm sorry, but I just can't do it." She offered a weak smile. "But, honestly, thanks for today. I'll remember it with pleasure…even this un-expectedly sweet goodbye.''

Before Adam could gather his thoughts, she'd slipped inside the house and closed the door behind her, shutting him outside with the seductive taste of her still on his lips and a delayed confusion settling over his brain. He stepped back, frowning at the dark house, waiting for a light to go on inside, signaling that she was safely havened within. Or maybe he was waiting for the light of understanding to dawn… because it had certainly sounded as if she'd just told him goodbye.

Not good-night.

Goodbye.

Coupled with her other statements, it could only mean she wasn't going to work for him and that she didn't plan to see him again. But that made no sense. She had to be aware—especially after today—that planning an event for his family, or any event con-nected with the Braddock name, would be advanta-geous for her business. She had to realize it would be a great experience, look enticing on a résumé, bring in new clients. She had to see it would be a plus any way she looked at it. He'd offered her an opportunity and a generous compensation for her ser-vices, so what possible reason could she have for turning him down?

Was she after more money? He encountered ma-nipulative people all the time, and money was always their bottom line. But Katie hadn't struck him as ei-ther manipulative or greedy. On the contrary, she'd seemed about as unimpressed by him so far as any-one he'd ever met. Plus, she'd sounded genuinely appalled when he'd suggested she wanted more money. Closing the door in his face just now wasn't exactly a smart negotiating ploy, either. She must know he could walk away and never look back. Why with a single phone call, he could have Nell tracking down every events coordinator in New England. And he could afford to hire every last one of them if he wanted.

But he didn't want every events coordinator in New England. He wanted the one he had.

Maybe he'd misheard her or was reading more into the words than was warranted. People said goodbye all the time without meaning anything final by it. Sometimes, too, people said they couldn't do something because they wanted to be persuaded that they could. Of course, it was possible she'd been intimidated by all she'd seen and heard today at the Hall, and her refusal was connected in someway to that.

Or maybe his impulsive kiss was to blame. Not that that made any better sense. Most women would read more into it than they should. That was one of the reasons he was always so careful about who he kissed...and when...and where...and even, how. He didn't like misunderstandings. So, okay, he hadn't been careful just now. He hadn't even been halfway prudent.

It had been a mistake to kiss her. No two ways about it. But she hadn't disliked kissing him. He felt it wasn't conceited to believe, based on the evidence, that she'd enjoyed it, too.

Benson cleared his throat and Adam realized he was still staring at Katie's front door like a bewildered suitor. Turning on his heel, he strode back to the car nonchalantly as if women rejected his offers all the time.

They didn't, and he couldn't recall the last time he would have cared. His last affair had been over for three weeks before he remembered to tell Nell to cancel his standing order of Monday morning flowers. Not that this was anything like that. He wasn't involved with Katie, wasn't going to *get* involved with Katie, wasn't even interested that way. Certainly, he wasn't going to be sending her any flowers.

But he'd be damned if he'd let her back out of her commitment like this.

At least not without giving him an explanation he could understand.

"EVERYONE'S READY for this to happen," Lara was saying. "Allen is available to go over the new contract with you whenever you want. I've gone over it with him three times and think it's vastly improved, but I know you'll want to make some suggestions. Wallace is plenty nervous now. The joke circulating among the team members this morning is that he's offering to sweeten the deal by throwing in his vacation home in Malibu, if you'll just agree to meet with him."

Adam swivelled his chair away from the panoramic view of the Providence skyline. "What would I want with a house in Malibu?"

Lara arched her eyebrows. "That's the joke, Adam." Her expression turned genuinely curious. "What is going on with you today? If I didn't know better, I'd think you hadn't listened to a word I've said."

"I listened." But he hadn't. Not really. His ability to tune out distractions had gone on the fritz and the only words that kept repeating in his ears were Katie's. *Goodbye,* she'd said last night. *I just can't do it.* Leaning forward, he punched the speaker option on his phone and jabbed in Nell's intercom number. "Have you reached her yet?" he asked without preamble.

"No answer," Nell said apologetically. "No way to leave a message. Do you want me to keep trying?"

"Yes, and ring through the minute you have her on the line." He clicked off the speaker and frowned at Lara, who was giving him an odd look. "What?" he asked.

"Just wondering who she is and how she managed to rain on your parade." Lara, tall, cool, beautiful, smart and more woman than most men could handle, was, perhaps, the only person who could read Adam accurately. She'd been his assistant for five years and worked even harder than he did. When he'd first hired her, Adam had thought a more intimate relationship was bound to develop between them, given their mutual passion for their work and the long hours they spent together. But the spark had never kindled, much less caught fire. Perhaps because they were two of a kind, and too ambitious to expend the energy needed to conduct an affair. Or maybe they were too selfish to risk the friendship that had grown like a weed and ended up a hardy wildflower.

Or maybe, as he often suspected, he'd had nothing to do with the decision at all and, from the start, Lara was simply wise enough to avoid that complication.

Either way, Adam appreciated her ability to read his mood and intuit his thoughts, even now, when he found it vastly annoying.

"She's the events coordinator I hired to put together a party for Grandfather's birthday." He tapped the heavy pen in his hand against a pile of papers on his desk. "And she told me last night she can't do it."

"Because…?"

"She didn't give a reason, just she can't do it."

"Idiot," was Lara's succinct reply.

He smiled. "I don't think so."

"She wants more money, then." Lara's thoughts, as usual, tracked his own.

"She says no."

"And you believe her?"

He did. Unbelievably this morning, he still did. "Yes."

"Offer her more, anyway."

He'd thought of that, too. "I don't believe it will make any difference."

"Money always makes a difference."

"I think she'll still refuse."

Lara shrugged. "So get someone else."

It was, of course, the obvious thing to do. "She came highly recommended."

"All of them do. You want me to call down to PR and get Kelly to put together some ideas for you to look at? She's done a great job with the last two company functions."

"You know how I feel about using employees for family matters."

"Okay, I'll find someone outside the office."

"Grandfather seemed very taken with Katie."

She leveled a narrowed gaze at him. "He's lonely, Adam. And I'm sure she's pretty."

"He is, and she is, but I hardly think either condition is relevant. It isn't as if he's looking for romance at his age."

"Don't be naive, Adam. He's a man, and even at his age, believe me, he's looking."

Lara was wrong. Adam had grown up in the shelter of his grandparents' devotion to each other. He knew there could never be another woman in Archer's life. He also knew Lara's own family had given her no reason to believe love could last a lifetime or grow deep, and strong, and solid through the years. He dismissed her concern, and other options, with a shake of his head. "Sooner or later, Katie is bound to answer her phone."

Lara pursed her lips and moved on. "All right, then. Obviously, you don't need my input on events coordinators. So what do you want me to tell Wallace's people?"

Adam didn't much care, which was an indication of just how bothered he was by Katie's inexplicable behavior. She couldn't *not* want to do this party. His grandfather had been on the phone to him twice already wanting to congratulate him on his choice and to ask when Katie would return to the Hall. Archer's enthusiasm was reason enough to keep ringing her number. "Friday," he said, making the decision. "I'll meet with Wallace Friday."

"Friday," Lara repeated. "Wouldn't Monday be better? Peter's coming in from Atlanta on Friday and—"

"Monday, then," Adam snapped, agitated for no good reason. "I don't know why you ask me when you already have the timing worked out in your head."

"It won't do our side any harm for Wallace to cool his heels over the weekend. Especially after the way he screwed with us last week."

"Has anyone ever accused you of being soft-hearted?"

Her smile was self-confident and sure. "Not more than once." Rising, she picked up the report they'd just gone over and tucked it efficiently in the crook of her arm. "Shall I send Allen in now?"

Before he could answer, the intercom buzzed. "Nell," he said, pressing the button to turn on the speaker phone. "Did you reach her?"

"I'm sorry, Mr. Braddock, no. I'm still trying. But your brother is on line one. I thought you might want to take his call."

"Which brother?"

"Mr. Bryce, sir."

Adam pressed the key to take the call. "I thought you were sailing with Holden," he said, apropos of nothing except he was angry that Bryce was on the line and Katie wasn't.

"We pulled into Locke's harbor at the Vineyard to stay tonight. Holden's mechanic persuaded him to get some new experimental winch installed and of course, it doesn't work, so we're here letting tempers cool. Hello, Lara."

"Hello, Bryce. How astute of you to know I was here."

"You're always in my brother's office," he said

in a voice that tormented just by its smooth delivery. "Eavesdropping on my phone calls to him is the only light in your dreary life."

"How thoughtful of you to want to brighten my day. I'm certain it's the first unselfish thought you've had all week."

If Adam and Lara had established an immediate rapport, Bryce and Lara had negotiated an even quicker hostility. Adam didn't know why his brother delighted in goading her, or why Lara didn't just ignore his jibes, but he did and she didn't, and Adam refused to play the peacemaker. "What do you need now, Bryce?" he asked.

"I *need* a phone number," Bryce said, his tone taking on a confrontational note. "Katie's phone number. You whisked her off so fast last night I didn't get the chance to get it."

"I don't have it," Adam lied. "Try the phone directory."

"Not listed."

He was happy to hear that. "Sorry to hear that," he said.

"Okay, if that's the way you feel about it, I'll just wrangle it out of Nell."

Lara smiled, the light of battle in her eyes. "You're stranded at the Vineyard and trying to phone a woman here in Providence? What's wrong, Bryce? Did they lock up all the nubile young women when they heard you were going to be in town?"

"Katie's worth a long-distance call," he replied, unruffled. "Ask Adam. He's smitten with her, too. Although I'm sure he'll deny it."

Adam avoided Lara's inquisitive glance and cut

off her retort. "This is a business office, Bryce, and a business phone, and Lara and I have business to conduct, so if there's nothing else, I'll see you this weekend at the Hall."

"Sure thing." If Bryce was bothered by Adam's rough dismissal, he didn't let it show in his voice. "Say hi to Katie for me." And he hung up.

Immediately, Adam regretted his brusque handling of Bryce's call. He missed the camaraderie they'd once shared and the brotherly affection that had somehow fallen prey to an unhealthy sibling rivalry over the past couple of years. He didn't know what had caused it or how to re-establish their friendship. He did, however, know there was no way he would ever pass Katie's number along to his brother. Not that it would do Bryce any good if he did since she wasn't answering her phone anyway.

"Katie." Lara's tone pondered the name, as if it were a great mystery. "Hmm," she said. "The plot thickens."

"Bryce flirts with every female within range," Adam said to set her straight. "He'd even flirt with you if you'd give him the slightest encouragement."

"Not even in an alternate universe." She seemed to relish the idea of banishing the middle Braddock brother to another, and probably evil, realm. "It's not his flirting with her that surprises me. If you did *whisk* her away from him, then apparently she made quite an impression on you, as well."

He liked Lara. He didn't know what he'd do without her razor-sharp intelligence and keen insights. That didn't mean he wouldn't fire her in a heartbeat if she crossed the line between business and personal once too often. "Set the meeting with Wallace for Friday," he said. "And tell Allen I'll see him now."

Being the fine employee she was, Lara heeded the warning and snapped into professional mode without a blink. "A morning or afternoon meeting on Friday?" she asked.

He smiled, softening the tone and allowing her some part of the decision. "I'll leave that to you."

"Afternoon, I think." She smiled, too, and walked briskly to the door. "Anything else?"

"Just Allen."

"He'll be here in five minutes."

Adam nodded, tapped the nib of his pen against the desk some more, and contemplated the idea that Katie was avoiding him. She probably checked the number ringing in, saw the Braddock name, and didn't answer. Or maybe she simply hadn't turned on her phone at all. For some reason, he believed she just didn't want to talk to him this morning. But why not? And if she wouldn't take his calls, who would she talk to? Whose call would she answer without a second thought?

Ilsa Fairchild.

Without a moment's hesitation, Adam jabbed the intercom. "Nell," he said. "Get Ilsa Fairchild's phone number for me, please. I'll hold." He waited, wrote down the number as Nell read it to him, then repeated it back to her.

"Do you want me to get her for you now?" Nell asked, all efficiency and barely suppressed interest.

"No, I'll do it myself. Better stop Allen on his way in and ask him to wait out there until I'm through talking to her."

He jabbed off the connection, and punched in the number, pleased to be taking some action, even if he had no idea what he would say to Mrs. Fairchild when she answered.

Something would occur to him, though. Katie owed him an explanation and he fully expected to have one before the day was over.

Chapter Five

The Torrid Tomato was packed with the usual boisterous lunch crowd, but as she followed the hostess to a booth in the back, Ilsa caught sight of Katie and waved.

Katie waved back and shimmied through an opening between two waiters to make a clean slide into the other side of the booth just as Ilsa was seated. "Mrs. If!" she said with a big smile. "I'm so glad you came in for lunch today. It's my last day of work here, can you believe it?"

Ilsa smiled back, delighted as always at Katie's joyful exuberance. "I love the new hairdo."

Katie touched a loose curl with fussy fingers. "Thanks, I just got it cut a couple of days ago and I'm still not used to it. I thought a shorter and sassier do would be easier to manage in the Southern heat."

Disappointment tweaked Ilsa's good humor. "So you really are leaving Providence?"

Katie made a face in answer. "That was the original plan, but the house I was supposed to take in Baton Rouge sold and the agency is frantically looking for something else for me. There was a place in

Phoenix and another in Tucson, but I was there in the middle of summer last year and, thank you very much, I'm in no hurry to go back. A little sun goes a long way in Arizona."

"I can't believe it'll be any cooler in Louisiana. Plus there is the humidity factor, you know."

"I've heard." She grinned. "Bryce Braddock told me and since he never lies about the weather, I guess it must be true."

Ilsa's eyebrows rose in surprise. "I didn't know you'd met Bryce."

"Bryce, Adam, *and* their grandfather. Of course, you introduced me to Adam a couple of weeks ago when you were in here having lunch with him, remember? Not that he does. Somehow, he's gotten me all mixed up with somebody else he must have met, but can't remember meeting and he's got this crazy idea that I'm some kind of events planner. When I try to tell him I'm not, he doesn't listen worth a barn owl's hoot. It's the most bizarre thing. I was going to tell you Monday at Tai Chi class, but since you're here now, I'll take my break and tell you the whole crazy story. You are *not* going to believe this, but probably a week or two after that day you had lunch with him, Adam Braddock called me and said you'd given him my phone number and recommended tha—"

"Katie!" An impatient someone in the kitchen yelled out. "Order up!"

With a grimace, she pushed out of the booth. "Got to go, Mrs. If, but I'll be back. Do you want me to put in an order for some artichoke dip?" She stood and leaned in, lowering her voice. "You didn't hear this from me, but stay away from the specials today. Kenny is in a really *un*creative mood.'' She rolled her eyes and was off to pick up and deliver.

Ilsa flipped open the napkin and smoothed it on her lap, thinking that Katie must have run into Bryce on her visit to Braddock Hall on Tuesday. Of course, Katie didn't know that Ilsa already knew about that trip, that she'd had not one, but two separate accountings. Ilsa knew from experience it was never useful to speculate on what might happen after one of her *Introduction of Possibilities,* as she'd come to call them, but she had been taken quite by surprise when Archer's phone call came. Certainly, she'd set up the lunch with Adam at The Torrid Tomato, and certainly, she'd noticed the spark when his eyes had met Katie's. And she had, purposely, made certain Adam had the business card with Katie's phone number on the back when he left the restaurant. But she couldn't, in a million years of matchmaking, have predicted that he'd somehow conclude Katie was a party planner and then offer her the job of planning Archer's birthday party.

But the unexpected was what made her work so interesting. It validated her personal belief that love would find a way against incredible odds. Of course, it was a long and winding path from possibility to happily ever after, as she'd tried to caution Archer. But he'd fallen in love with Katie on the basis of that one afternoon, declared she was the perfect match for his eldest grandson, and could hear nothing but wedding bells pealing madly in the near future. Ilsa wasn't that optimistic, although she had been encouraged when Adam phoned to ask for her assistance. He wanted her to persuade Katie to take on the task of planning Archer's party. Something more than a sit-down dinner for two hundred was on the line, Ilsa could tell that by the intensity in his voice and in the quite stunning fact that he'd called her himself instead of having his secretary do it.

Pleased by the hopeful turn of events, Ilsa smiled at her waiter, ordered a glass of tea, a plate of quahog stuffies, and waited eagerly to discover Katie's take on Adam Braddock. It would, of course, require diplomacy to listen without revealing all she knew about Katie's visit and Adam's agenda, but that was, after all, one of the things she did exceedingly well. She hadn't lied to Adam or to Katie and she wouldn't. On the other hand, she saw no good reason to correct the impression each had formed about how, exactly, Adam had gotten the number of Katie's cell phone.

If their relationship unfolded in the same wonderfully mysterious way it had begun, by the time they figured out their misconception, it really wouldn't matter one way or the other.

WHEN ILSA FAIRCHILD suggested Adam talk to Katie in person, it had sounded like a reasonable idea and the obvious way to proceed. On the way to Katie's house, when he spied a street vendor and impulsively asked Benson to stop, taking a gift of flowers had seemed like a perfectly sensible, gentlemanly thing to do. But now that he was standing on her front porch, holding a bouquet that seemed, by turns, overzealous, wildly inappropriate and way too personal, he wondered what had gotten into him.

He wasn't courting Katie. He just wanted her to work for him. Right now, however, *that* seemed like the worst idea of all. Just because his grandfather had taken a shine to her was no reason for Adam to be on this doorstep now. He didn't need a party planner this badly. He didn't even *like* parties, for crying out loud. He'd just turn around, get back in the car and go to his four o'clock meeting with Wallace.

Adam turned to leave, hesitated, turned back. Okay…he'd ring the doorbell. He'd come this far. He might as well ring the doorbell. Once. Not that he expected her to answer the door any better than she answered her phone.

His finger was poised over the backlit button, ready to push it, when the front door was flung open and Katie stood in the doorway, staring at him as if he were the creature from the Black Lagoon.

"Adam?" she said, as if she wasn't certain.

"Katie." His tone was just right, he thought. Businesslike. A bit cool. Impersonal. Not at all nervous, which was, remarkably, the way he felt.

She looked at the flowers then back to his face. "What…what are you doing here?"

"Your phone must be out of order. I've been trying to call you for days."

"Days," she repeated vaguely and her gaze dropped again to the flowers. "I just saw you Tuesday."

"All right. I've been trying to call you for two whole days and a large part of this one."

She frowned, crossed her arms low across her waist, then uncrossed them and smoothed the shirttails of her white blouse. "Um, sometimes I don't answer my phone."

"That's an unusual way to run a business," he said, thinking this wasn't such a bad idea after all. She was clearly rattled by his presence at her door, which for some reason made him feel better about being here. "I wouldn't think it would be very profitable."

"No, I…uh…guess it isn't." She was wearing a pair of denim shorts that showed a surprisingly long, tantalizing expanse of leg—shapely leg—and her feet were bare, a slender silver ring glinting around one toe. He didn't even want to think about why he found *that* appealing.

"An answering service might be a good idea," he suggested. "For those times when you can't take your calls. That's even available as an option with your cell phone service."

"Hmm." Her dark hair curled in charming disarray around her face and her eyes were bluer even than he remembered. He wondered if she'd thought much about the kiss they'd shared right here on this porch and if she was wondering if he might be about to kiss her again. The possibility had occurred to him about half a second after she opened the door.

"Were you on your way out?" he asked before possibility became impulse and, from there, disaster. He was here to hire her. Period. End of fantasy. "I hadn't even pressed the doorbell yet."

"I saw the Rolls through the window and thought I must be imagining…" She blinked and seemed to gather her composure. "What *are* you doing here, Adam?"

"Mrs. Fairchild suggested I stop by to see you."

Katie seemed surprised at that. "She told me I should give you a call...or at least answer the phone when you call."

"Most of the time, it was my secretary phoning. Nell."

For the first time, a hint of a smile touched her lips. "I sorta figured that." She contemplated the bouquet again. "When did you talk to Mrs. Fairchild?"

"Right after she had lunch with you today."

Her eyes met his. "I've only been home an hour. You weren't allowing me much opportunity to take her advice."

"Were you going to call me?"

"I hadn't decided."

He pressed for more of an answer. "But you were leaning toward...?"

"Probably not."

He frowned, his bout of nervousness giving way to frustration. "I don't understand your attitude, Katie. Grandfather's birthday party represents a great opportunity for your business. There's no good reason for you to pass it up because you feel it may be more of a challenge than you're used to tackling."

"I'm not afraid." Her chin came up with the words. "I just don't think it would be right, that's all."

"If it's because I kissed you the other night, I can assure you it won't happen again."

She regarded him thoughtfully, her head tipped to one side, assessment mixed with a wry humor in her eyes. "It has nothing to do with that. Look, there must be a hundred people in Providence who'd love to work this event for you. Why not hire one of them?''

"Grandfather likes you. He's being very insistent that this is his birthday and you're his choice to handle all the party arrangements." He softened his tone, offered a wry smile, knowing they'd come to a crucial moment in the negotiations. "It would mean a lot to me and to my brothers if you'd reconsider your decision." He paused, then gave it a little push. "I seldom ask for anything twice, Katie."

Katie took a deep breath and held it while she argued with her better judgment. She wanted to do this. Her whole body ached with the desire to test her mettle against Adam Braddock. Which was, mainly, the problem. After his kiss, she couldn't pretend the sizzle she felt every time she looked at him was harmless. He might have convinced himself that one kiss would be the end of it, but she was wise enough to know the attraction would develop into more kisses and more…well, a whole lot more. Especially if she had anything to say about it.

But she was ready to leave Providence—as soon as the agency found a place for her to go. It didn't matter that she'd already quit her job, that she was in limbo for the time being. The important thing to keep in mind here was that she was ready to move on to the next adventure of her life. Getting involved with Adam, even temporarily, was not just bad timing but a complication she didn't need. She'd said as much to Mrs. If today at lunch and been surprised by her friend's laughing response. *Are you avoiding complications, Katie? Or possibilities?*

"Are you all right?" Adam looked at her with concern.

She let her breath out in a rush. She might be a lot of things, but a coward she wasn't. "I'm fine," she said, deciding to take the possibility of adventure he was offering and wondering not for the first time why he hadn't left the flowers in the car. They were already wilting in the afternoon sun. "You really should have those in water," she said. "They're going to be all dried out and dead by the time you get wherever you're going."

"What?"

"The flowers." She pointed to the bouquet he seemed to have forgotten he held in the vise of his fist. "They aren't looking too healthy."

He frowned and appeared slightly embarrassed as he jostled the tissue-wrapped stems. "Great, and here I was counting on them to swing the sympathy vote my way."

"Sympathy vote?"

"All right, so it's a bribe...a last resort to help my cause."

"You mean they're...for me?" She couldn't believe he'd brought flowers for her.

"For you." He extended the bouquet toward her and she gathered it in like a pleasant memory. And truthfully, she couldn't remember the last time anyone had given her flowers. And for a cause, too. She buried her nose in their sweet fragrance.

"Mmm," she said. "Thank you."

"So you'll reconsider? About the party?

She tipped up her chin, offering a coy smile into

the bargain. "You've been watching too many FTD commercials."

His hand came up, passed warmly across her cheek, nestled in her hair, and caused her heart to stop beating. "You've got a daisy caught in your hair," he said. "Don't move."

As if *that* were an option. Her heart picked up speed, racing to recover the missed beats and it was all she could do to keep her head from leaning into his touch and betraying her sudden lusty yearning with a provocative gesture.

"Sssshhh," he said, but whether he was soothing her, the curl, or the snagged petals of the daisy she didn't know.

She felt a tug, a ripple of *possibilities* all the way from her head to her toes, and then the flower and the curl were freed.

"There." His smile proved he was even more handsome than she'd remembered. Just when she'd convinced herself he'd been merely a nice-looking man, here he was. The very definition of handsome. "A lucky escape."

For the daisy maybe. She, on the other hand, was caught, but good. "I'd better put these in some water," she said and turned back into the house. "Come inside." She sensed, rather than saw him glance at his watch. "Unless you don't have time."

He stepped inside, probably because she hadn't actually uttered the magic words that meant he could mark *party planner* off his to-do list.

"I'll just get something to put these in," she said, heading for the kitchen. "Make yourself comfortable." She heard him close the door and felt the quiet

FREE GIFTS!

NO COST! NO OBLIGATION TO BUY!
NO PURCHASE NECESSARY!

DETACH AND MAIL CARD TODAY!

PLAY THE
Lucky Key Game

Scratch gold area with a coin.
Then check below to see the books and gift you get!

354 HDL DH2T
154 HDL DH2K

YES! I have scratched off the gold area. Please send me the 2 Free books and gift for which I qualify. I understand I am under no obligation to purchase any books, as explained on the back and on the opposite page.

NAME   (PLEASE PRINT CLEARLY)

ADDRESS

APT. #   CITY

STATE / PROV.   ZIP/POSTAL CODE

| 🔑🔑🔑🔑 | 2 free books plus a gift | 🔑🔑🔑 | 1 free book |
| 🔑🔑🔑 | 2 free books | 🔑 | Try Again! |

The Harlequin Reader Service® — Here's how it works:

Accepting your 2 free books and gift places you under no obligation to buy anything. You may keep the books and gift and return the shipping statement marked "cancel." If you do not cancel, about a month later we'll send you 4 additional books and bill you just $3.80 each in the U.S., or $4.21 each in Canada, plus 25¢ shipping & handling per book and applicable taxes if any.* That's the complete price and — compared to cover prices of $4.50 each in the U.S. and $5.25 each in Canada — it's quite a bargain! You may cancel at any time, but if you choose to continue, every month we'll send you 4 more books, which you may either purchase at the discount price or return to us and cancel your subscription.

*Terms and prices subject to change without notice. Sales tax applicable in N.Y. Canadian residents will be charged applicable provincial taxes and GST.

If offer card is missing write to: Harlequin Reader Service, 3010 Walden Ave., P.O. Box 1867, Buffalo NY 14240-1867

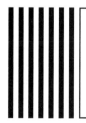

BUSINESS REPLY MAIL
FIRST-CLASS MAIL   PERMIT NO. 717-003   BUFFALO, NY

POSTAGE WILL BE PAID BY ADDRESSEE

HARLEQUIN READER SERVICE
3010 WALDEN AVE
PO BOX 1867
BUFFALO NY 14240-9952

NO POSTAGE
NECESSARY
IF MAILED
IN THE
UNITED STATES

of the house fold around them in an intimate privacy. Maybe she should have invited Benson in, too.

"Nice house," he said when she returned to the front room with a galvanized watering can, filled with flowers that were already regaining their vigor.

Setting the improvised vase on the coffee table, she looked around. "A little too symmetrical and a lot too beige for my tastes, but nice enough, I suppose."

"So none of this is yours?"

"Nope. I'm baby-sitting the whole kit and caboodle." She gestured him to a seat and couldn't decide if she was disappointed or relieved when he chose a chair positioned a safe distance from every other possible seat in the room. The sofa was directly behind her, so she dropped onto its beige cushions and tucked one bare leg beneath her. "That's usually the way this house-sitting arrangement works. Most of the time, it's a house that's been on the market for a while and just needs a lived-in look to sell. Sometimes the furniture is rented. Sometimes it's been left with the house. Sometimes, it belongs to the house-sitter. Sometimes, it's the property of the leasing agency. Once in a while, like with this house, the owners had to be away for six months and contacted an agency for a sitter." She shrugged. "They got me."

"What do you do with your furniture and all your other things when you're house-sitting?"

"I don't collect things. Just experiences."

His expression turned skeptical. "A nice sentiment, Katie, but not very practical. I know, for instance, that you collect books. Large, heavy books."

"I buy quite a few books, true, but I only collect the experience of reading them, then I give them away."

"But you must have clothes, personal items—" his gaze tracked pointedly to the watering can vase, "—whimsical articles to make you feel at home in a strange place."

"Whimsy can be found anywhere, and no one really needs a whole closetful of clothes." She shrugged, knowing Adam wasn't likely to ever understand her philosophy of life or the obligation she felt to explore every facet of life. "I travel light."

His eyes narrowed. He was still, obviously, unconvinced. "You must have some sort of business office. Or at least a computer."

She shook her head.

"A desk, a chair, an appointment book, pads of sticky notes? I know you have a phone."

"A cell phone," she admitted. "A necessary concession to safety and convenience in this day and age."

"Well, it would be if you'd answer it." He glanced at his watch again and she knew his thoughts were already divided and on their way somewhere else.

"I suppose it would never occur to you to let a phone call go unanswered?"

"Of course, it occurs to me," he said. "Unfortunately, there aren't that many I can afford to miss." As if to illustrate the point, a phone rang and he pulled a high-tech, *Star-Trek* communicator look-alike out of his pocket and flipped it open. "Yes, Lara?"

Katie flexed her legs and shifted position, tucking both legs into a half-lotus, pretending not to notice that her action had caught Adam's attention. He watched her even as he listened attentively to someone else, a circumstance she found both titillating and disconcerting. The undisguised interest in his gaze sent a dangerous quicksilver thrill down her spine. She was an idiot to pursue this. She knew it in her normally, very, self-protective soul. He was so out of her league, she might as well have been born on another planet. But some core of loneliness in him echoed a loneliness she tried never to acknowledge inside herself, and she knew she was past the point of listening to reason on this one.

"I'll be there in fifteen minutes." Adam was on his feet, addressing his remarks to the cell phone, his attention diverted away from Katie and back to the absent Lara. Agitation showed in his voice and in the overall tension of his body language. "Give him some more coffee. Ask him what he thinks about the Celtics. Get him to talk about his family. Have Nell ply him with cookies or brownies or peppermint tea or something. I don't care. Just don't let him leave before I get there. I don't understand why he showed up an hour early. Are you sure you told him four o'clock?" A pause. "All right, but for now, just do what you have to do to keep him there. We'll find out who's responsible for this mix-up later." His goodbye was a sharp metallic *clack* as he snapped the phone case shut.

Katie was ready for him when his scowling gaze flicked to her. "Now aren't you sorry you answered that call?"

He didn't seem to see the humor. He didn't even seem to be aware he was talking to her and not just to himself. "Wallace again. I'm don't know what kind of game the man is trying to play, but it's wearing very thin with me."

"It must be scary to sell a company you've built from the ground up."

"Wallace does not need your sympathy, believe me. He'll be more than well compensated for his trouble. He'll never have to worry about working another day in his life."

"And that must be the scariest part of all."

Adam frowned. "Well, this deal is going through if I have to put on a Halloween mask and scare the living daylights out of him myself." His scowl cleared as he tucked the phone into the breast pocket of his suit coat. "I have to leave. Please tell me now if you'll take the birthday event or not." He paused to offer an engaging smile. "And remember…you did accept the bribe."

"So I did." She looked at the flowers, then at his expression which was, at least momentarily, intent on her answer. She wondered what kind of heroic measures it would require to distract him from the places he had to go and the things he had to do. With a sigh, she acknowledged that distracting him was a long shot at best and not at all likely to be in her own best interests. "I know I'm going to regret this—and you probably will, too—but okay, I'll do it."

The remaining furrows in his forehead vanished and his smile flashed with a pleasure she felt as if it were her own. "I'm glad." He offered her his hand

and she let him enclose her fingers in a hearty deal-clincher of a handshake across the coffee table. A zinger of a hot flash traveled from his touch up her arm and zapped her heart with a warning. Too late, of course, to be of any use. Her common sense always had to play catch-up with her free spirit. "I hope," he said, "that this means you'll answer your phone now when I call you."

"When you tell Nell to call me, you mean."

He smiled. "It might not always be Nell. You'll have to answer to find out."

"Well, either way, I'm not making any promises. I've got about a million things to do in the next few days, myself." He was moving toward the door and she trailed after him. "The couple who owns this house is coming back Sunday and the place I was supposed to move into sold. Now that I've let you persuade me to take this birthday party gig, I'll need to find somewhere else to stay in Providence. All of which means that if I'm out looking for a place to hang my hat, I may not be able to keep my cell phone fully charged and ready for your call."

"Stay at the Hall," he offered, opening the door. "There's plenty of room and it isn't even an hour's commute. I'll put Benson and the Rolls at your disposal." He stopped, looked down at her, and a sweet, sensual longing filled the air, like the scent of a fragrant flower. "Plus, if you're there, I won't have to track you down somewhere else."

Proximity, proximity, proximity. If there was one thing she should definitely *not* do, it was stay in too close a proximity to him. "That's probably not a good idea,'' she said, intending to tell him she'd find something else—a safer, saner place to stay.

But he leaned in, as if he were going to kiss her, and she forgot why it had seemed important to say anything at all.

''I'll send Benson to pick you up. When do you have to be out of here?''

Mesmerized by the nearness of his lips, by the proximity of his whole body, she gulped and whispered, ''Tomorrow.''

''Benson will be here at noon.'' He straightened with a smile. ''Don't forget to pack your party dress.''

He spun on his heel and was striding toward the car before she had time to blink, much less consider what she'd just committed herself to do. Well, she'd just have to take her chances under the auspicious roof of Braddock Hall and keep her eyes and heart open to the possibilities she might discover there. She'd plan the party to the best of her ability and when it was over, she'd take only the amount of money she felt was a fair wage for her labor—depending, of course, on how the party turned out—and move on.

After all, how hard could it be to plan a festive, everyone-has-the-time-of-their-life birthday party? With a generous, if not unlimited, budget, even a person who had to start from scratch ought to be able to put together enough food, flowers, fun and fandango to satisfy a couple of hundred guests. Adam hadn't specified the kind of party he expected. Truthfully, he didn't seem to have any stipulations past the point of getting her to agree. Why he wanted her,

Katie couldn't even begin to guess, but if he'd asked Ilsa Fairchild to come into the restaurant today for the express purpose of aiding his persuasive efforts— and he apparently had—he'd been determined to gain her services one way or another. Of course, Mrs. If hadn't *said* that was her reason for coming in, and she certainly hadn't expressed an opinion either yea or nay. On the other hand, she had offered to help with contacts or advice should Katie decide to take on the challenge. So why, Katie wondered, shouldn't she wade into this adventure the same way she did everything else—with enthusiasm and the basic expectation that everything would work out just fine. Even if it turned out badly, the experience would be good for her.

Which was the thing about collecting experiences, good or bad, she was stuck with them. She couldn't decide to clean house and just sell off the experiences she didn't want to keep for a penny a pound at a yard sale. But even as she watched the Rolls-Royce pull away from the curb and speed toward downtown, Katie knew there was a better than even chance that this time around, she could wind up wishing she collected Beanie Babies, instead.

"THERE WILL BE a guest arriving tomorrow afternoon, Abbott." Adam made an initial sort through the stack of mail the butler had designated as worthy of his attention. "Her name is Katie Canton and she'll be staying with us for a few weeks." He frowned at a glossy envelope and slid his thumb under the seal to open it. A wedding invitation. *Sarah Angela Merchant.* Wasn't she the debutante Peter had been dating just a few months ago? Sam, he'd called her. Or maybe Angel. Apparently, they weren't seeing each other anymore. "Make sure Ms. Canton has anything she needs, Abbott."

"Very good, sir." Abbott was of the old school of butlers, proper, professional and proud. "Shall I put her in the room next to yours?"

Adam looked up, caught unawares by the butler's diplomatic question. "No, of course not," he said, then realized Abbott needed some basic information. "Ms. Canton is the events coordinator who will be planning Grandfather's birthday celebration. You met her Tuesday. She was here to look around the grounds."

"I remember," Abbott said. "A delightful young woman."

"Yes," Adam agreed absently. "Now that I think about it, she might enjoy a room in the north ell. What do you think?"

"The guest rooms there have a lovely view of the gardens, sir, and the added advantage of being as far away from the family quarters as possible and therefore…quieter."

Abbott, who knew family secrets even Archer probably didn't, knew exactly what Adam was suggesting. No point in being diplomatic. "Bryce isn't staying past Sunday, is he?"

"I don't believe so, sir, but it's difficult to know with Mr. Bryce. His plans are often subject to change without notice."

Adam frowned, shuffled through the mail again. "While Ms. Canton is our guest, you'll please keep me informed when my brother's plans change without notice."

"I will, sir." Abbott nodded his understanding. "And Mr. Peter? Shall I make you aware of any change in his plans as well?"

"I don't think..." Adam stopped. If he was assigning himself the role of chaperon, he might as well play it full out. "Yes, Abbott. If Peter's plans change unexpectedly, please make sure I know about it."

"Checking up on me, Adam?" Peter Braddock descended the stairs at a trot, his unruly dark hair newly cut short and in the latest, trendiest style. His clothes were straight out of *GQ* magazine, right down to the blue sports coat flung casually over his shoulder. Peter was nothing if not photogenic. "Don't you have better things to do?"

Adam looked up, taking in his youngest brother's faultless appearance with a raised eyebrow, but making no comment. "Hello, Peter. How was your trip to Atlanta?"

"If you're asking about the building project, my report is on your desk. If, on the other hand, you're interested in my personal impressions of the city, I'll give you the highlights at dinner." He reached the bottom step and set foot in the foyer with a purposeful two-step. "Aren't you home early? I thought you had a meeting with Wallace late this afternoon."

"We were supposed to meet at my office at four o'clock. He showed up at three, claiming someone in his office had phoned and changed the time for the appointment. By the time I got back, it was a quarter of four and he was long gone."

"Where were you?"

"Taking care of something else," Adam said, not sure why he felt defensive about it and still amazed that he'd actually invited Katie to stay at the Hall. It had seemed a harmless suggestion at the time, a nice gesture to make, but almost before the car door closed behind him, he regretted the impulse and wished he'd given her the chance to say no.

"Looks like Wallace isn't as anxious for this deal to go through as we want to believe." Peter let the jacket slide from his shoulder and caught it smoothly in the crook of his elbow. "Could be he's getting cold feet about taking that early retirement."

It was what Katie had said, too. But Adam was still hot over the missed meeting and didn't want to think about Richard Wallace and what might, or might not, be his problem this time around. "What are your plans for the weekend, Peter?"

"You don't seriously believe I'm going to tell you that, do you?" Peter laughed and clapped Adam on the upper arm. "If I so much as mention I have five minutes free, you'll have me in your office discussing the layout and design of the Atlanta building…and then you'll expect me to spend the rest of my weekend sketching out changes. No thanks. This is a *family* weekend, remember? You, me, Bryce, Grandpop…Dad."

"Dad?"

Peter nodded. "Must be time for us to be introduced to our next and future stepmother because Abbott tells me they're on their way and will be staying with us until after Grandpop's birthday."

This was news to Adam and he looked to the butler for confirmation. "Mr. James and his fiancée, a Ms. Monica Labelle, should arrive at the Hall sometime tomorrow," Abbott verified. "It is my understanding they will both be staying through the celebration."

You see? Peter's shrug said with eloquence. "Ten to one, Ms. Labelle convinced him to renovate the Colorado house before the wedding and she's allergic to the smell of paint. Either that, or she's thinking she can persuade him to move here so we can all be one, big, happy family."

Adam knew that was highly unlikely. James and Archer didn't see eye to eye on much of anything, hadn't for years, and the tension ran abnormally high whenever the two of them resided under the same roof. Consequently, James's trips to Braddock Hall tended to be infrequent and usually of short duration. He'd long ago made a life for himself elsewhere and with limited contact, he got along pretty well with his father and three sons. Most of Adam's memories involving his father centered around holidays and an occasional vacation trip of one sort or another.

And the weddings. Adam and his brothers were always invited to the weddings.

"What a pleasant surprise," Adam said drily.

"Kind of makes you wish the Hall came equipped with a separate guest house, doesn't it?" Peter winked at Abbott, whose spine stiffened in response. Abbott had never known quite what to make of the youngest Braddock brother. Perhaps because Peter had been a strapping nine-year-old when he came to live at the Hall and more than a little rough around the edges. Grandmother Jane deserved a great deal of credit for turning that graceless, often sullen pre-teen into this self-confident and sophisticated young man. Abbott deserved a medal of honor for putting up with him. "Which Step-mommy Dearest will this one make, anyway?" Peter asked. "Are we at lucky thirteen, yet?"

"Number six, I believe." Adam didn't like to think about the number of marriages, and subsequent divorces, James had gone through in the past few years. Reason enough that his three sons—all born to different mothers—were cautious about making commitments themselves. "You may want to see this." He pulled the glossy wedding invitation out of the stack of mail and handed it to Peter. "I expect you're the Braddock who is most particularly invited."

Peter took the card and read it in a glance. "Ah, Angel. I knew her well. Send my regrets, please, Abbott?" He passed the invitation, round-robin, to the butler. "I've got to clean my aquarium that weekend."

"You don't have an aquarium," Adam pointed out.

"I'll get one, then."

"Weren't you and Ms. Merchant something of an item just a few months ago?" Adam tried to recollect the occasion. "I thought she was the blonde you had on your arm at the Winston's holiday ball."

"That was Samantha Herrmann," Peter corrected. "Angel was my date for the Harvest Gala last October. I can see where you'd be confused, though. They're both tall, blond and very lovely."

An apt description of every woman Peter dated.

While Bryce considered all women equally worthy of his attentions, Peter was more selective. He liked them tall, blond, lovely and privileged. Only blue-bloods need apply for the honor of appearing on Peter Braddock's arm. "So," Adam probed. "How is Samantha these days?"

"Couldn't tell you, Adam." Peter pulled a set of car keys from his pocket and gave them a casual toss. "Haven't seen her since I took Miranda Danville to the Valentine's Day benefit."

"Another tall, lovely, blonde." Adam sighed and pulled a couple of envelopes from the stack of mail before handing the rest to the butler. "Good thing the events planner I hired for Grandfather's birthday is a spunky, little brunette."

"Who's to say the right brunette couldn't change my mind about blondes in a heartbeat?"

"This brunette is off-limits. I don't want you or Bryce distracting her from her work or filling her head with the idea she should take your flirtation seriously."

Peter's brows winged upward in surprise. "Well, well, well, Abbott, what do you make of this ultimatum? Sounds to me as if I'm being warned away from my big brother's new amour."

The word had a strange allure, but Adam ignored it to give his brother a warning look. "Don't be ridiculous."

"Sorry," Peter said, although he didn't sound as if he meant it. "How soon can I meet her?"

"Tomorrow. She'll be staying at the Hall until after the party."

Peter looked doubly surprised at this unprecedented happening. "Now that's an intriguing setup."

Adam wanted to explain that it was mere convenience and that there was no intrigue to it, but further explanation would only invite more, rather than less, speculation. Katie wasn't Peter's type. She wasn't Bryce's type, either, but that wouldn't stop either brother from giving her the idea they'd each been waiting for her all their respective lives. "Isn't it?" he countered. "And I'd appreciate it if you and Bryce would consider her off-limits."

Peter's brows went even higher, and his frank curiosity filled the sudden silence with a new speculation. Belatedly, Adam realized his offensive strategy might have unanticipated side effects. He was almost glad when the phone on the credenza rang and Abbott moved efficiently to answer it, breaking the tension and diverting Peter's attention. "Oh, I forgot to tell you, Adam," Peter said. "Mayor Henry called earlier this afternoon. Also Belle Yeager and Jules Jackson. I think you've skirted the Christmas decoration issue only to find you're knee-deep in bricks." With a grin, he headed for the door. "I'll be back in time for dinner."

"It's Mayor Henry, sir." Abbott looked to Adam for instruction. "Do you wish to take the call?"

Bricks? Adam thought as he nodded and motioned Abbott to transfer the call into his study. Whatever was brewing in the Sea Change cauldron wasn't likely to improve his day. The Wallace deal seemed to be slipping through his fingers. And the news that James was bringing home yet another soon-to-be Mrs. Braddock filled Adam with an uncertain dread.

There was no reason he should be anticipating to-morrow and the weeks leading up to his grand-father's birthday with such unexpected pleasure.

No good reason, at all.

Chapter Six

Katie stepped into the large corner bedroom, thinking even Alice in Wonderland might have felt a little overwhelmed. The room, like the rest of the house, was gracious, luxuriously elegant and oversized, with ceilings so high even an NBA star would have to have a tall ladder to change a lightbulb. It was as lovely a bedroom as any Katie had ever slept in and easily ten times the size of the cubbyhole of a room she'd occupied during the eleven years she lived with her grandparents in Oklahoma. "Wow," she said. "You could billet a whole Boy Scout troop in here."

"There's a great view of the gardens from this room." Adam set her duffel and two bulging shopping bags on the floor. "And a pleasant cross-breeze in the evenings at this time of year."

Katie walked to the window and looked out in an effort to hide the fact that she was as nervous and excited as a half-grown pup on a visit to a tree farm. Over the past twenty-four hours, she'd had long talks with herself and a couple of brief conversations with Ilsa Fairchild. By the time Benson arrived in the Rolls-Royce, Katie had her shoulders squared, her chin up and a *can-do* attitude tucked securely in her heart's pocket. She'd been fine with the whole party-planning, see-what-life-is-like-inside-the-manor adventure...right up until the moment Adam had made a proprietary snatch of her duffel bag and staked some kind of claim by declaring to the butler and Ruth, the housekeeper, that *he* would personally escort her to her room. Which he'd done. "It is a beautiful view," she said.

"When I was a boy, my grandmother would plan camp-outs in different rooms of the house. I think she wanted to be sure we knew our way around and wouldn't get lost in our own home. This room was always one of her favorite campsites."

"No campfires allowed, I take it?"

"We're pretty careful with fires around here. The original Hall was built in 1834, but burned in 1870. It was promptly rebuilt, and burned again in 1915. When the house was rebuilt then, the fire retardant features were the best money could buy. Needless to say, they've been updated many times since. No point in taking chances."

"What did you do on the camp-outs with your grandmother?"

His smile went soft with memory and caught at her heartstrings. "Learned about family history, the responsibilities of being born a Braddock, the duty of stewardship. Of course, I didn't know that at the time. Grandmother was a wonderful storyteller and I thought we were only having fun."

"You and your brothers?"

"Just me, at first. Then Bryce arrived and joined us on the in-house excursions. By the time Peter came to live with us, though, I was long past the point of enjoying a camp-out.''

"Peter wasn't born here?'' she asked, surprised.

"My father was the last Braddock to be born here at the Hall. I was born in Boston, while my parents were students at Harvard. Bryce was born in Dublin, Peter in California.''

"Your mother must have liked to travel.''

"My mother died when I was born,'' he said. "Bryce's mother, I believe, is still living in Ireland. Peter's mother died several years ago. You've probably read that much in the tabloids. From time to time, the whole story of our father's many wives surfaces again. You'll meet him...and his fiancée...at dinner this evening.''

Katie heard the undertones, knew this was a sore subject. "I'll look forward to it. Does he live here?''

"Colorado. Braddock Industries owns several up-scale shopping centers around the country and he heads up our management company there. He prefers to be closer to the mountains than the ocean.''

"I like mountains,'' Katie said, turning again to the view out the window, mainly because he had such a startling effect on her ability to breathe in and out in a normal fashion. "I like the ocean, too. If I had to choose, though, I think I'd always want to be wherever there's a garden.''

His steps were muffled by the thick, wool carpet, but she knew the moment he stopped a couple of feet behind her, felt an internal shift...as if her body leaned unconsciously toward him like a flower to the sun. "I've asked Abbott to set up a little office for you in the adjoining room. There should be a phone, fax, computer and a few other essential business items. If you need anything else, tell Abbott and he'll get it for you.''

''I may need a guide to find my way downstairs again.'' A giggle escaped her tight throat, a squeaky nervous sound. ''Are all the bedrooms in this part of the house?''

''The seven bedrooms on this north ell are the guest suites. The eight bedrooms in the north ell are for the family and occasionally for guests, too.'' He paused, seeming almost nervous, himself. ''I thought you'd have fewer...distractions here.''

She would if he stayed out of her bedroom. ''This is perfect,'' she said, keeping her eyes on the garden because looking at him was dangerous. ''The gardeners could prove distracting, though. What are they doing to that rhododendron?''

He stepped in closer to see the two men who were in the garden below, one of them bronzed and bare from the waist up, one of them in a broad-brimmed straw hat. ''I don't know, but the one in the hat is my grandfather. The other one is Peter.'' There was an oddly awkward pause. ''I can't imagine why he's taken off his shirt.''

''He must be hot.'' Katie leaned forward in the window to get a better look at Adam's youngest brother. ''Or working on his tan.''

''It's more likely he didn't want to get his shirt dirty. Peter is something of a clotheshorse.''

''Hmm,'' she murmured, wondering what it would take to get Adam to take off his shirt. ''He should consider going without more often. He's very nicely cut and buffed.''

"Cut and buffed?" Adam's tone was suddenly frosty, but she didn't know if it was because Peter wasn't wearing his shirt or because she'd noticed.

"That's girl talk for well-built." She glanced over her shoulder and realized he, obviously, knew that already. "Your brother has a nice body," she finished lamely.

The room temperature dropped ten degrees in a split-second. "I'm sure he'd be pleased to know you think so but, despite depriving you of a nice *view,* he should not be in plain sight of your window without a shirt."

She blinked, baffled by his attitude. "Guess this is just my lucky day."

"After tomorrow, I shouldn't think you'll have much time for distractions of any kind. Abbott will provide you with a guest list for the party first thing Monday morning. If you have any questions, ask my grandfather. He's the one in the hat, in case you didn't notice." Adam was at the doorway almost before she had time to frown at the sharp rebuke in his voice.

She'd done nothing to merit this brusqueness and couldn't let it go unchallenged. "I intend to ask him about the rhododendron first chance I get. On second thought, though, I may just go out there now and ask Peter, instead."

That stopped him, brought him turning back toward her with a narrowed, somber look. "Ask Grandfather," he said with much more authority than was necessary. "Cocktails are in the library at seven and we dress for dinner."

"I never doubted it for a second." She smiled

winningly. "Although in your brother's case, it does seem a shame."

"Keep your focus on the birthday party, Ms. Canton. That's the reason you're here. I advise you not to forget it." He spun on his heel and was out the door, closing it quietly and very firmly behind him.

Katie sagged against the windowsill and stared at the door. Perplexed didn't begin to describe her state of mind. What on earth was wrong with the man? He'd invited her here, practically insisted she come, but from the moment she'd stepped through the front door, he'd behaved...well, like a nervous suitor. Anxious, eager, confiding, distant, brusque. And all within the space of the thirty minutes—max—she'd been in his house. Even now, his reaction to her perfectly harmless remark was way out of line, almost as if he were...jealous. But that was crazy. She hadn't even *met* Peter yet. And why would Adam be jealous, anyway? He couldn't be offended because she found his brothers attractive. That was silly. They *were* attractive. She'd have to be blind not to notice. He'd warned her not to take Bryce's flirting serious. Maybe he was warning her about his younger brother, too. But there was no need to be so highhanded about it. Or maybe he was issuing a general warning to her not to get any ideas about her stay at Braddock Hall being anything but temporary.

Well, he was in for a surprise if he thought she was looking for anything permanent. And if she were, this was definitely the last place she'd look. He was definitely the last man she'd consider, too. Him, or his brothers. Shirts or no shirts. She looked back out at the garden, at the maze of spring flowers, the wide expanse of lawn, and at the thicket of forest beyond. Okay, so maybe this wouldn't be the last place. And maybe Adam wouldn't be the last man.

He was as unnerved by her presence in his home as she was by being in it. Possibilities were bouncing all over the place and just because Adam wanted to pretend they didn't exist, didn't mean she had to agree with him. The attraction was there. It was real…and she didn't think it was just going to disappear because he was uncomfortable with it. As for herself, she'd still like to have his undivided attention for an hour or so…just for the experience. And if the opportunity arose—in more ways than one—she intended to carpe diem.

The gardener guys were out of her range of sight now, so with one last sympathetic smile for the now-uprooted and presumably soon-to-be-moved-to-another-location rhododendron, she went to look through the shopping bags. She'd gone on quite a spree yesterday. In leaving one place and heading toward another, she normally changed her wardrobe. She'd found it was more practical than toting winter clothes to Phoenix or dragging a sundress to Minnesota. When she was ready to leave an area, she donated her better clothing items to a woman's shelter and bought what she needed once she arrived at her next destination. But yesterday, instead of shopping exclusively at the upscale resale stores she normally favored, she'd taken some money from her savings and purchased some brand new outfits. It was a small concession to the Braddocks' affluency, but one she was already glad she'd made. However, if dressing for dinner was an everyday occurrence, she was probably going to need even more clothes. But too many, she believed, was as bad as too few and she did not like to be wasteful. After all, she was only going to be here a few weeks. So she'd just make do with what she'd brought, and should a fashion emergency arise, she'd follow Adam's instructions and tell Abbott.

After all, she was here for the whole experience. Wasn't she?

SHE'D DRESSED FOR DINNER.

Adam felt his jaw go slack when Katie walked into the library. He imagined every other male in the room had the same reaction, although he couldn't take his eyes off of her long enough to check. It would be downright un-American not to appreciate the red dress—what there was of it—and the narrow strip of white lace ribboned like a necklace around her throat. Her shoulders were bare except for the sheath's tiny, spaghetti-thin straps. Not that the dress needed straps to hold it in place. It clung, not too tightly, but not loosely, either and there wasn't an inch worth of slack in the fabric anywhere. His gaze took the path of least resistance, following the line downward to her legs which, he noted, were bare. And long. And lovely. And she was—to his astonishment—barefoot.

Adam didn't know whether to take off his coat and wrap it around her shoulders or just stand back and admire her toe ring.

James, never at a loss when a beautiful woman made an entrance, was at her side in a heartbeat, introducing himself and offering to get her something to drink. Bryce, a real chip off the old block, put the drink—a wine spritzer—in her hand almost before the request was out of her mouth. Peter, never one to rush, wowed her first with a *GQ* smile and then moved forward to be introduced.

With little more effort than simply walking into the library, Katie bewitched them all. But with a commendable sense of timing, she allowed only a few moments to pass before she turned her attention to Archer. As the family patriarch, he deserved the deference of her greeting and the honor of her conversation. His own greeting was warm, welcoming and eager, his eyes brightening at the sight of her. Adam's doubts about the wisdom of having Katie at the Hall lessened. But only a little.

By the time Monica, a petite brunette, arrived on the scene, her thunder had already been stolen. Her perfectly proper black dress seemed lackluster and dowdy next to Katie's simplicity of style and vibrant color. The sparkle of diamond drops around her neck and on her earlobes looked gaudy contrasted with the ingenuity of Katie's lace adornment. There wasn't anything natural about the dark shade of hosiery Monica wore on her legs, either. Even her strappy, three-inch high heels looked overdone and pretentious. By the time James greeted his fiancée with a kiss and introduced her to Katie, it was clear to Adam that Monica was not a happy camper.

"Couldn't decide which shoes to wear, Katie?" Monica asked in a thick, syrupy accent. "James is all the time teasing me about having so many pairs it takes me a month to choose which ones to wear." She smiled up into his handsome face. "I think it would serve him right if I followed your example and didn't wear any at all, don't you?''

Katie looked down at her bare feet and brought her gaze up with a self-deprecatory laugh. ''I didn't think my Birkenstock sandals did much for the outfit, and my Old Maine Trotter deck shoes looked even worse, so this isn't so much a choice as the lesser of the evils.''

''You *surely* didn't bring only *two* pair of shoes?''

There was a pause. ''I surely did,'' Katie said, proving she could hold her own against a Southern accent. ''In fact, I only own two pair of shoes. Imagine that.''

Monica clearly couldn't. ''You don't mean it. I never knew any woman who didn't have at least a dozen pair.''

''Well, congratulations. Now you do.'' She dazzled the assembled and attentive Braddocks with a wide smile, Adam included. ''I'm starving,'' she said. ''How long until dinner?''

From there, Katie owned the evening. She could do no wrong. In one brief, civilized encounter, she'd refused to be patronized and introduced a heretofore unknown concept under the Braddock dinner table— barefoot casual with a silver toe ring.

LARA SAT FORWARD in the chair, laying her hand flat and decisively on Adam's desk, eagerness in every nuance of her being. ''I say that while Richard Wallace *rethinks* his decision to sell his company, you stop playing Mr. Nice Guy and authorize a takeover. The whole team is ready to move on this and wondering why we haven't done it already.''

Adam looked from his assistant to the attorney seated next to her. "Allen?"

"If we're going to do it, now's the time, Adam. There's a rumor on the street that Dutton is going to make a move on the Wallace Company if our deal falls through." Allen shrugged, an action meant to disguise that he was as eager for the kill as Lara. "My guess is we have until the end of the week to make a decision, one way or the other."

Adam nodded, wondering why he couldn't work up any enthusiasm for this strategy or even any particular affront at being called a *Mr. Nice Guy*. Maybe because he was thinking hard about something else. Shoes. Bare feet. Long legs. Nice body. Wide smile. Blue eyes. Dusky hair. Silky curls. Katie. And right back to shoes again. Or rather…no shoes.

He couldn't seem to stop thinking about her bare feet. She'd been barefoot at breakfast on Sunday morning, too, because, she'd said, who wanted to put on shoes first thing in the morning? He didn't know how she felt about wearing shoes at noon because Bryce had hijacked her midmorning and took her off to see his collection of sailboats. Adam didn't know if she would have worn shoes at dinner that night either, because before he even realized plans for the evening were afoot, Peter had whisked her away to a party at Rorie Reynolds's house. It wasn't unusual for Peter to socialize with the local crowd. He'd come to the Hall from an entirely different environment and culture and was as comfortable with the kids in town as with any of the teens on the social register. There wasn't a thing wrong with that, of course, simply another part of his youngest brother that Adam had never quite understood. But, be that as it may, he didn't like the idea that Katie had spent the whole day out with his brothers instead of getting right to the work she'd been hired to do. He'd thought she would want to spend at least a part of the day with him, talking about plans for the party. But neither he, nor the job she was at the Hall to do, seemed to be uppermost on her mind.

The following morning, he'd left early, driving himself and leaving Benson and the Rolls for Katie's use. He'd thought of at least half a dozen items she might not realize needed immediate attention, so he had Nell send a fax as soon as he arrived at the office. When no reply was forthcoming, he had Nell phone. No answer, so he had Nell send another fax. By ten o'clock it was clear that either the phone lines to Katie's suite weren't working, or she was ignoring his suggestions, or she wasn't there to answer either phone or fax. He instructed Nell to call Abbott, who would find Ms. Canton and instruct her to phone Adam at his office, immediately if not sooner.

It was after one when Nell returned with the information that Ms. Canton was out. Adam fumed, wondering which of his brothers had stolen her away from her party planning duties today and if, perhaps, she was thinking she could parlay her job into a permanent change of address and last name.

Ridiculous, of course. Neither of his brothers was looking for a long-term relationship, merely a temporary diversion. But Katie might not realize that or she might believe she could bring about a change of heart. She could have wrangled the invitation to Braddock Hall with plans to snag one of the elusive brothers in matrimony or at least, a compromising position. She might believe she could steal James—probably the easiest Braddock target—out from under Monica's trim little nose. It was even possible she thought Archer was fair game for a savvy, mercenary little party-planner. After all, Adam really knew almost nothing about Katie and much as he hated to agree with Monica about anything, it was odd for a woman to have only two pair of shoes.

"Adam?"

He came back with a start to the inquiring frown on Lara's face and Allen's quizzical expression. "I'm thinking," he said because he was, although not about business. He couldn't recall ever having so much trouble concentrating. Nor had he ever spent much time worrying about who his brothers happened to be romancing. But something about Katie bothered him.

Okay, so it was more his own attraction to her that bothered him. That and a nagging sense of familiarity he still had not been able to place. Then, just when he managed to push those concerns aside, a very unsettling suspicion that one or the other of his brothers would have Katie in bed within the week returned to distract him. Just the thought of her with Bryce...or Peter turned his stomach into a churning knot of agitation and jealousy.

No, not jealousy. Of course, it wasn't *that*. He was feeling a simple—and understandable—concern at the possibility of trouble stirring under his own roof. This party to celebrate his grandfather's birthday was important, a milestone. Who knew how many more birthdays Archer might have? Who could predict how many more events the Braddock family would be together to celebrate? No, this party had to be one they would all remember with pleasure, and not because of an ill-conceived and ill-timed romance. It was bad enough that James had brought yet another unremarkable fiancée home for the occasion.

A soft, almost soundless sigh reached his ears and Adam felt the impatience pace about his office like a caged tiger. He knew Lara wanted his answer, was biting her tongue to keep from asking him what was taking so long. He knew that in her mind, his decision was a foregone conclusion. Business was business and Richard Wallace had thumbed his nose at Braddock Industries. And that, to her, was not just incomprehensible, but unforgivable.

But when he pushed his thoughts toward the business at hand, they took a fast slide toward home base, returning like a boomerang to Katie and the trouble he had inadvertently invited into his home with her. But was she really such a threat? So his brothers were attentive to her. So what? They were all grownups, for the most part, and Katie was one of only two women present at the Hall. Since the other one, Monica, was off-limits and of limited interest, anyway, it was only natural Bryce and Peter would choose to flirt with Katie. A psychologist would probably say that with their father flaunting another, obviously doomed-for-failure relationship in their faces, it was perfectly understandable they would shower any available other woman in the house with extra attention.

As for the rest, sooner or later he would remember where he'd met her before. And so what if she had only two pair of shoes? She'd told him she collected experiences, not things, and as odd as the concept was, when coupled with her all-embracing approach to life, it sounded normal. Right, even. He was wasting his time imagining trouble where none existed. Why, it was ridiculous to think Katie had manipulated him or anything else about the situation. He'd pursued her like a madman, hadn't given her an opportunity to refuse either the job or the invitation to stay at the Hall. And his speculation was not only pointless, but a waste of time.

He had inherited his grandfather's ability to read a man's character in a handshake and a relatively small amount of conversation. He had learned from his grandmother the art and integrity of trusting his feelings. He was seldom wrong about the people he met and he knew he wasn't wrong about Katie. She was special in a way he couldn't quite define and honest all the way down to her ten bare toes.

There was, he decided, nothing to worry about.

Except, perhaps, why he could not get the persistent and tantalizing image of Katie's bare feet out of his head.

"Wallace won't take a call from me?" he asked, before Lara's silent frustration grew even louder.

"He's unavailable," she said succinctly, her tone indicating it was not the first time this information had been given. "No matter who's calling."

Okay, so it was decision time. Adam turned his chair to look out the windows at the always lovely, usually soothing, view of the Providence River. For some reason, he had no taste for a cutthroat takeover. Maybe, as Katie had innocently suggested,

Wallace wasn't looking forward to retirement. The man had developed his company out of sheer grit and determination. He'd worked indecently hard all his life. Maybe *not* working was a more fearful prospect than holding on to a company that had outgrown his ability to manage successfully.

Adam tented his hands and tapped his thumbs together in a debating rhythm. One decision down. One to go.

"Offer Wallace a position in development," he said without turning around.

There was a pregnant pause before Lara's astounded, "What?" filled the office.

"You heard me." Adam continued to face the window, monitoring the progress of a shell as it was propelled through the water by a team of oarsmen.

"In *our* development department?" Allen asked, clearly hesitant about the idea.

"He won't want to come to us, so set this up as a whole new department through the manufacturing company. Put him in charge of the whole idea. Tell him we want him to work on improving the extrusion process for the steel." Adam swivelled back to face his disapproving audience. "I believe that will take care of this final roadblock."

"*Final* roadblock?" Lara wasn't pleased. "I think you're overly optimistic, Adam."

Strangely enough, he did feel optimistic all of a sudden. Very optimistic. "I know you'd prefer a more aggressive approach, but that's my decision." Command was implicit in his voice and both Allen and Lara got to their feet immediately, ready to carry out his orders.

At the door, Lara looked back. "You have to admit, a hostile takeover would be more fun."

"For some, more than others." He smiled and came to a second decision. "Lara? Where do you buy your shoes?"

ADAM ARRIVED at the Hall with four pair of ladies' size seven—he'd guessed at the size—shoes and feeling ridiculously proud of himself. The feeling changed fast enough when Abbott informed him that Ms. Canton, along with the rest of the family, had gone into Boston for the day. Even Mr. Archer had taken the trip. And no, Abbott wasn't expecting them to be back for dinner. He believed, in fact, it had been mentioned that they were going to try a new restaurant.

By the time he finished his own solitary meal, Adam was back to being certain he'd made a huge mistake by inviting Katie to Braddock Hall. An even bigger mistake by being so presumptuous as to buy her shoes. *Shoes.* What the hell was wrong with him? Well, whatever was wrong with him had started the moment he'd dialed her number. Or maybe it had started when he'd kissed her so impulsively on her porch. Didn't matter. He was ending this nonsense here and now. She was here to plan his grandfather's party and he was going to make certain that's what she did. If he had to supervise every moment of every day she spent in this house, then that's simply the way it would have to be. From now on, he'd make certain she was so busy putting the party together that she had no time to gallivant off to Boston for the day, or go sailing with Bryce, or run off to parties with Peter...or to do much of anything else.

And first thing tomorrow, he was sending the shoes back to the store.

KATIE HAD THREE DRESSES. A short red one with spaghetti straps. A small blue print, also short, with cap sleeves. And a brief black number with a modest scooped neck and a kicky, inch-wide black and white checked taffeta ruffle around the bottom...to keep it from being ordinary. Combined with, respectively, a white sheer blouse, a sparkly, silver-threaded cotton sweater, and a versatile, multi-colored silk scarf, she could create a variety of different looks. All of them, she thought, suitable for an evening with the *we-dress-for-dinner* Braddocks. She intended to buy shoes, she really did. But on Sunday, she went with Bryce to Newport during the afternoon and to a party at Rorie's house with Peter that evening. For both excursions, her Birkenstock sandals were fine with her navy capri pants and the aforementioned cotton sweater. On Monday, there was an impromptu trip to Boston—at Archer's suggestion—and they didn't return until late. On Tuesday, she borrowed Ruth's bicycle and rode into Sea Change, only to find herself right in the middle of a heated discussion between Betina of Betina's Cut and Curl and Ethan of Sea Change Antiques right in the middle of the Town Square. Betina, considered a newcomer since she'd only owned the beauty salon six measly years, and Ethan, who could trace his roots clear back to 1679, were at odds over a proposal to repave Dockside Avenue with bricks, sidewalks and crosswalks included. Betina and her supporters thought the bricks would lend a sense of history and cozy, small-town flair. Ethan and his constituents said, *"Nonsense."* In their view, Sea Change had plenty of real history and was cozy enough as it stood, cracked pavement, deteriorating sidewalks and all.

By the time the discussion ended in a draw, Katie had forgotten about shoes altogether. So that night, when dressing for dinner, she took a length of blue ribbon, laced it loosely around her big toe, looped it twice around her ankle, crossed the strands under her instep and tied it in a perky bow on top. She repeated the procedure on her other foot and thought it was a rather ingenious solution to a temporary problem. But when she saw Adam looking at her feet, not once, but a bunch of times…when she noticed the way he tried not to let her see that he'd noticed her footwear…when she felt the sizzle as his eyes met hers and skittered away as if her gaze burned his…well, she began to rethink the idea of buying shoes. Why spend money on something she didn't truly need when the Hall had lovely smooth floors and nice, thick wool carpet and, as a bonus, a man who couldn't seem to keep his eyes off her.

Katie had never felt particularly clever when it came to seduction. For one thing, she hadn't had much practice. For another, she thought the invitation ought, as much as possible, to be a mutual thing. Somehow, though, she couldn't see Adam Braddock initiating such an invitation to her. He was fighting this attraction too hard. But she knew she wasn't the only one to recognize the *sizzle* that ricocheted between them every time their eyes met. And it was not her imagination that the early threads of awareness were growing increasingly stronger, pulling them persistently, irrevocably together like the weaving of an intricate design.

Katie had no idea if anything would come of it, had a thought that Adam might not allow the attraction to run its course, whatever that course might be. But there were still three weeks left before the birthday party and she was in no hurry. So if her being barefoot unsettled him, threw him a little off-balance, and got his mind out of his briefcase for a few minutes every evening...well, why would she stop? In her, admittedly, biased opinion, Adam needed less responsibility and a whole lot more fantasy in his life. Someone needed to be his fantasy woman.

Might as well be her.

At least, he'd be a better man for the experience. She could practically guarantee it.

SHE WAS WEARING ribbons on her feet.

Adam couldn't believe it. He couldn't stop looking at them either. Even when they were tucked out of sight under the massive mahogany dining table, he couldn't stop thinking about them. He had no idea even what was served for dinner. Capon? Duck? It could have been raw oysters for all the attention he paid to what he ate. By the time coffee was served, he decided it was time to put a stop to this barefoot nonsense, once and for all.

He hadn't returned the shoes. It had seemed somehow too foolish to buy them one day and take them back the next. It wasn't exactly the sort of thing he could ask Nell to do, either. So now he wouldn't have to return them at all. He'd give them to Katie, as he'd originally intended, tactfully suggest it would be best if she'd wear something other than ribbon or jewelry on her feet when she came to dinner, and thereby solve both his discomfort and her embarrassment at having only two pair of shoes.

It never once occurred to him that she might not appreciate his thoughtfulness.

Chapter Seven

Bryce barely tapped on Adam's bedroom door before opening it. "Have you seen Katie?" he asked.

Adam frowned at the intrusion and went back to buttoning his shirt. "She's not in here."

"That much I already knew," Bryce said, grinning. "Let me rephrase the question. Do you know where Katie might be?"

"My hope would be that she's in her office hard at work on Grandfather's party, but my guess is that since she isn't with you, she must be with Peter."

"Peter's in Boston. He left Sunday." Bryce entered the room, glanced at Adam, then walked straight into the closet, talking as he went. "If you'd been at dinner the past two nights, you'd know that."

"Someone has to work around here."

"What?" came the muffled reply from inside the closet.

Adam pitched his voice to carry his words and his frustration into the closet. "I have to work to keep you in wine and winches."

Bryce strolled back into the room, carrying a red silk tie, an easy grin still benignly settled on his handsome face. "I appreciate it, too, big brother, but I don't think Katie would like being called a wench."

"I was referring to a winch for your sailboat," Adam said tightly. He'd been in a foul mood for a week now. Ever since Katie had wrapped ribbons around her feet and come to dinner. Ever since she'd told him what he could do with his four pair of ladies' shoes. "Katie doesn't seem to like being called a party-planner, either."

"You're just mad because she's not doing this the way you would."

"If I'd wanted to plan this party, myself, I wouldn't have hired her to do it."

"Sure you would have. You like to *think* you hire an individual to do a job, but the truth is, you want worker bees who buzz around doing a thing exactly the way you would do it yourself. I hate to be the one to disillusion you, here, Adam, but you're the quintessential *my-way-or-the-highway* king." Bryce held up the tie against his yellow plaid sports shirt. "Do you think this is gaudy enough for the club? They have that rule about wearing ties in the dining room, you know, but I never like to be too conventional."

Adam frowned heavily at his brother in the mirror. "That combination should certainly make your point. Don't you have ties of your own?"

"None that go with this shirt." Slinging the tie across his shoulder, Bryce turned back to Adam. "I'm taking Katie to lunch at the club. You want to come along? Give her advice on what she *ought* to be doing instead?"

"A tempting invitation," Adam said, stuffing his

shirttails into his suit trousers with more insistence than necessary. "But as I mentioned, I'm working today. Unlike you...or Katie, apparently."

"Why should I work when I have you to do it for me? As for Katie, she's been working like a trouper, Adam. Ask Grandfather. Ask Dad, if you can get him away from Monica long enough for him to complete a whole sentence. Katie's even been spending her spare time in town, trying to mediate a temporary truce on the repaving issue before Saturday, just so the only question you'll have to contend with at the council meeting is the Christmas decorations."

"She should stay out of local politics and concentrate on what I brought her here to do." Adam fastened his belt and picked up his tie—a conservative, navy-and-cream print—already laid out with the suit for his convenience. "If I'd known she was going to be this much trouble..."

"What trouble? She's taking care of the party, she's friendly, she's polite, she doesn't eat with her fingers, she's fun, a good sport and she always has a smile for everyone. Even you. Despite the fact that you've been growling like a bear with a sore paw ever since she set foot in this house."

"She comes barefoot to dinner," Adam said before he could stop himself.

"She does?"

"Don't tell me you haven't noticed." He moved to the mirror to check the knot of his tie.

"Maybe I have, but isn't that beside the point? Katie is the first bit of sunshine we've had in this place since Grandmother died. Grandfather is almost like his old self again, laughing and whistling while he putters around in the garden. I even heard Abbott humming a showtune the other day.''

''I hardly think Katie can take credit for all that,'' Adam said, although he, too, had noticed a general uplifting of spirits around the Hall. Except for his own. He wished he could relax and enjoy the spurt of frivolity that followed Katie around like a playful puppy. But someone had to be responsible and make sure things got done and that job, as usual, fell to him. Jerking out the too-tight knot, he started over retying the tie. ''Especially as she spends most all of her time entertaining either you or Peter, which, as difficult as this may be for you to believe, is not what I'm paying her to do.''

''If I didn't know better, Adam, I'd think you were jealous.''

''*Jealous?*'' he repeated. ''Of whom? You?''

''Yes,'' Bryce said. ''Me. Peter. Anyone who receives the slightest bit of attention from Katie.''

Adam laughed without humor and slid the new, improved knot securely between the starched points of his shirt collar. ''Believe me, I am not jealous.'' Which was a huge lie. He knew it all the way to the pulsing green center of his heart. Ridiculous as it was, impossible as he wished it were, he was so jealous he could hardly see straight. ''And if I were,'' he said, calling up a cool, indifferent tone as he reached for his jacket, ''you can be sure I'd simply steal her away from you.''

Bryce laughed. ''I would *love* to see you try.''

''You don't think I can?''

''No, I don't think you'd take the risk of finding

out that you could.'' Bryce headed for the door. ''Thanks for the tie.''

''I want it back,'' Adam called after him.

Bryce stopped in the doorway, flipped the end of the red tie in a challenge. ''You get the girl,'' he said with a shrug, ''you get the tie.'' And with that bit of brotherly provocation—and the tie—he left.

SUBTLETY DIDN'T WORK. Katie had tried her best smiles on Adam. She'd tried listening attentively when he talked. She'd tried initiating conversation of a more personal nature than how much shrimp the caterer would bring and the last count of acceptances on their RSVPs. She'd tried eye contact and the *almost* accidental touch of her hand on his arm. She'd tried everything she could think of short of flat out propositioning him…and even if she wanted to try that, she'd probably have to make the initial offering via phone. Or by fax. If it wasn't electronic or didn't come out of his briefcase, the man just wasn't interested.

She was afraid she might have hurt his feelings over the shoes. But he'd taken her completely by surprise with his whispered, *''I have something to give you later.''* She'd thought—well, never mind what she'd thought. But never in a million years had she expected to open her bedroom door later and be presented—by Abbott, to add insult to injury—with four shoe boxes, each containing an expensive pair of ridiculously impractical—although pretty—shoes. ''Mr. Adam said you needed these,'' the butler had said.

Wrong. Wrong size. Wrong reason. Wrong

woman. She'd sent back the boxes, the shoes, Abbott and a note. *Please,* she'd written. *Give these to someone in genuine need. I have two pair already.*

But on reflection, Katie had wondered if she hadn't been too quick to take offense. He'd undoubtedly meant well, even if he should have known better. But she just couldn't like the idea that he'd decided she *needed* something and gone out and bought it for her. She didn't like that she'd told him she collected experiences, not things, but that what he'd *heard* was she needed things she couldn't, or wouldn't, buy for herself. She didn't like the underlying presumption that she wasn't up to Braddock standards if she wasn't wearing the latest style of leather on her feet. And she especially didn't like that he found her bare feet not scintillating, or sexy, or even simply interesting, but in *need* of shoes. She wanted, somehow, for him to accept her *as is* and not break his neck in his haste to conform her into a Monica, complete with the latest trend in high heels and the snooty attitude of ownership that went with them. That was the real reason she couldn't accept the shoes. Regardless of his intention.

She'd put on the Old Maine Trotters the next night because, obviously, it bothered him for her to go without shoes. But then, after a moment of second thoughts, she took them off again before going downstairs. If Adam objected to her bare feet, well, he was just going to have to talk to her, state his reasons, face to face, in person and in private.

He didn't.

Oh, it wasn't that he didn't talk to her. He did. He just never let the conversation drift to her feet. He wasn't home a lot but, when he was, he always seemed to have something to discuss with her. In his study. In private. Although Katie couldn't figure out why privacy was required since they merely talked for a few minutes about the party—if she were having any problems, if she needed any advice from him—and then, as if he'd been waiting all day for the opportunity, he'd begin telling her about the Wallace deal, what was happening, how things were progressing, and what he hoped this merger would mean for Braddock Industries. He seemed to want to know what she thought, too, although he never came right out and asked for her opinion. At times, she suspected he was trying to figure out if her advice about Wallace had been a fluke or if she really had some special insights. Other times, she was convinced he was playing dodgeball with the attraction that continued to sizzle between them, but which he seemed determined to ignore. When he never picked up a single one of her hints that she wouldn't mind if he pursued the attraction, she decided he was simply baby-sitting her so his brothers would have limited opportunities to pursue her. It was, she thought, exactly the sort of thing Adam would do. The kind of thing he'd feel it was his duty to do. It apparently didn't occur to him that she wasn't interested in his brothers. Or that she spent an inordinate amount of time thinking about him, remembering what he'd said and how he'd said it, and wishing he'd stop talking and start kissing her instead. So with a sigh of regret for what she thought might have been a lovely little interlude, Katie wrote off her attraction to Adam Braddock as a lost cause.

Which was why, when she answered a knock on her door one evening, Adam was the last person she expected to see. Certainly not with a picnic basket in one hand, a quilt tucked under one elbow, and a smile that made her knees weak. She couldn't decide if she was more surprised that he was there or that he wasn't wearing a tie. Or that the top two buttons of his shirt were left undone to reveal a glimpse of manly chest. Or that he'd rolled the sleeves of his white shirt midway up his forearms with a casual lack of precision…although it was a good look for him. Unassumingly masculine. Sexy. Very sexy. His appearance, on all counts, astounded her. But there he was…out of uniform and looking for all the world as if he hadn't been ignoring her for days.

"Hi," he said.

"Hi," she answered, cautious. This could be a trick. There could be shoes in that basket.

"I thought we might go on a picnic." He held up the basket, as if she might not have noticed it.

"A picnic," she repeated, wondering what this guy had done with the *real* Adam.

"That's right," he said.

"You and me," she questioned evenly. "On a picnic."

The lazy curve of his smile deepened. "That's what I had in mind when I asked Abbott to pack this basket."

"Just the two of us?" She wanted to be sure he wasn't asking her *and* the fax machine. "Alone?"

His gaze dropped tantalizingly to her breasts, lingered just long enough to interfere with her breathing, then came back to her face. "Unless you have a mouse in your pocket."

"The only mouse in this bedroom is attached to a computer...and if it's going, I'm not."

"Good, it's settled. The computer stays and you, Katie," his voice dipped to a husky bass, "are coming with me."

Whoa there, Nellie. She cooled the sweet, hot rush of her skittering pulse with a healthy dose of skepticism. So the man was quite literally charming her socks off. Didn't mean she had to capitulate without *some* show of spunk. "I *was* just about to go downstairs for dinner." She pointedly glanced down at her bare feet. He pointedly didn't.

"We finally made the deal with Wallace today, thanks in part to your suggestions, and I thought," he paused, the slightest hint of a shy hesitancy threading through his eagerness, "I hoped you might help me celebrate."

Katie recognized the Braddock charm at work. She'd been busy observing this family of males for almost two weeks now and she knew they could be powerfully persuasive. But either Adam was better than the rest of them put together or she was more susceptible to his particular brand of charisma. Dangerously susceptible.

"Congratulations," she said, trying for a prudence she was a long way from feeling. "Are you having it gift-wrapped?"

He seemed lost for a moment in looking at her. "I'm sorry, what did you ask me?"

"The company," she said, feeling foolish. "You

said you were getting your grandfather a company for his birthday and I said—''

''Was I having it gift-wrapped.'' He finished the sentence for her, nodding, bringing his thoughts back around from wherever they'd been. ''Somehow a company—even one so complementary to our own—doesn't seem like a very thoughtful gift now. Maybe I'll get him a tie.''

''Now that I know him a little, I think he'd prefer it if you gave him an afternoon.''

''More thoughtful, certainly. But also difficult to gift-wrap.''

''The best gifts often are.''

He leaned a shoulder against the doorjamb, as if he had all the time in the world and didn't want to rush her, as if he'd known her acceptance was a foregone conclusion the moment she'd opened the door to his knock. ''So,'' he said. ''You'll come with me?''

''On a picnic,'' she said to confirm it one last time.

''Yes.''

''Just the two of us.'' She wanted to be doubly sure what she was agreeing to before she launched out on this adventure.

A rakish angle appeared at the corner of his smile. ''I only packed enough champagne for two.''

''Abbott, you mean.''

His eyebrow went up in a question. ''Abbott?''

''Abbott packed the basket, so technically *he* only put in enough for two.''

''No,'' Adam corrected. ''I went to the wine cellar myself and picked out the bottle. I'm not a huge fan of champagne, but this is supposed to be a *very* good year. Trust me, we won't want to share this with anyone else.''

Trust me. Uh-huh. The plot thickened. She crossed her arms and ran her fingertips across the sleek fabric of her red dress as she considered what he was really after and whether she should go along for this little ride, or call his bluff right here and right now. ''You know, Adam, you don't have to ply me with champagne to get the latest head count for the party. It's two hundred forty-three and climbing.''

His brow lowered with a frown. ''I thought we only invited two hundred guests.''

Aha. ''I knew the real Adam was hiding behind that picnic basket somewhere,'' she said.

His smile was slow in coming, but so worth the wait. ''I'll make a deal with you, Katie. Unless you want to talk about it, the birthday party and any plans you've made for it are taboo subjects tonight. I promise I won't be the one to mention it.''

''That's a pretty rash statement for a guy like you to make.'' She was intrigued by the possibility he wanted to discuss something other than business with her...and by his very flirtatious manner. Something, clearly, was on his agenda. ''A picnic is bound to last an hour, at least, and that's a long time for you to spend with me, talking about anything that isn't business.''

His shoulder—the one not leaning casually against her door frame; the one attached to the hand that held the infamously mysterious picnic basket—lifted in a shrug. ''An hour's hardly any time at all, but if that's a challenge, I accept.''

His tone was softly persuasive, seductive,

even…and she—fool that she was—had already turned to putty in his hands. If he actually touched her, she'd probably fall in a soft, mushy clump at his feet. "It wasn't a challenge at all," she said, rummaging for her backbone. "But, as they say, if the shoe fits…"

A poor choice of words, she realized too late. But he merely laughed when she winced. "Shoes are optional on this picnic…as on most all other occasions. I believe I owe you an apology, Katie. I've never known any woman with your sense of…style."

There. Simple. Direct. An apology of sorts. But with no justification offered. And certainly no admission of being in the wrong. She took a small measure of offense at his tacked-on *"style"* and used it to stiffen her elusive backbone. But still, she was truly perplexed by this overall change in his behavior, and couldn't think of any explanation for it. Well, she could think of one, but much as she'd like to, she couldn't really believe he'd suddenly fallen victim to her charm and decided to seduce her on the spot. "Maybe I should put on a pair of shoes. We might have to cross a stretch of rocky ground to get to our picnic site."

"Go barefoot. If the going gets rough, I'll carry you."

Her heart caught at the idea of being in his arms, skipped a beat and rushed on ahead of her imagination. "Well," she said. "In that case, what are we waiting for?"

With his free hand, he captured her fingers and folded them within the warmth of his palm. "I was waiting for you to say, yes." Turning easily, he drew her out into the hall with him and reached in to close her bedroom door behind them. There was a certain finality to that...as if he was symbolically closing the door on the past week and leading her down a hall-way that was dim, but led to brighter spaces. Or maybe she was just being overly optimistic as she walked beside him down the hall, her hand securely held in his, their soft footfalls accompanied by a large anticipation and a faint, crystal *clinking* sound from inside the picnic basket.

"Should we stop off in the library to let the family know we won't be at dinner?" Katie asked.

"No," he said definitely. "Abbott knows, and as for the rest, I expect they'll be able to guess we're together."

Katie didn't see how. "Maybe I should stop and tell Bryce, just as a courtesy. He said something earlier about going for a drive after dinner."

"There's no need to do that. Bryce will know you're with me."

There was something about the way he said it. A satisfied note in his voice, a certain tightening along his jaw, a quickening of his steps. "And why will Bryce jump to that conclusion, Adam?"

He glanced at her and kept walking. He also kept hold of her hand, but perhaps he squeezed it a bit more tightly. "He just will, that's all."

She got the picture. Clear as morning on the ho-rizon. Two brothers. One woman. This wasn't ex-actly rocket science. She stopped walking, let her hand slip free of his. "This is some kind of contest, isn't it? A competition. Which Braddock brother gets the girl tonight. Isn't that what this sudden change of attitude represents, Adam?''

He stopped, seemed to consider how to answer. Then, decisively, he set the picnic basket on the floor, turned to face her in the dusky hallway and put his hands gently, but firmly on her shoulders. ''Bryce dared me to try and steal you away from him, yes. He also accused me of being jealous, which I denied. But I've thought long and hard about it, and concluded he's right. I've behaved badly this week. I could tell you my mind was on the Wallace deal. I could make a dozen excuses, all with some basic element of truth. But the reason—the *only* reason— I'm here now has nothing to do with Bryce or Peter…and everything to do with simply wanting to be with you.''

It would take a stronger woman than she was to stand against a statement delivered with such flattering simplicity and innate charisma, whether he meant it or not. She was already half in love with the man as it was, despite—or maybe because of—the fact that he had tried so hard to resist her and this optimistic, tenacious attraction between them. Not even a glimmer of attraction sparked when she looked at either of his two brothers. Bryce was amusing and an all-around nice guy, but while she knew he liked her, his flirting wasn't serious. It was merely a diversion, a way to emulate his father and aggravate his older brother. As for Peter…well, he was still too much in search of himself to be interested in her and from the moment they'd met, he had treated her as if she were his sister, certainly never as a potential lover.

But Adam...well, that was a horse of a different color altogether. The little shiver of excitement that swirled down her spine every time their eyes met, every time he even walked into the same room, made no sense. Certainly, it had no future. But if she prided herself on living in the moment—and she did—ready or not, this was it. She'd promised herself she'd be open to possibilities during her stay at Braddock Hall and a possibility had just opened up like the petals of an exotic flower, blooming where it had no business even being.

Raising on tiptoe, she moved against him and kissed him impulsively, and fully on the lips. There was no teasing in the kiss, no tantalizing lures. She wanted to promise him—and herself—no more than this one moment. It was meant to be just a simple, honest kiss, a way of saying that she recognized the attraction and was open to the possibility of it. But with the touch of their lips, it instantly and unexpectedly became a covenant. There was more here than she'd bargained for and Katie was suddenly, completely aware of it...and afraid of losing a part of herself she'd never intended to put in jeopardy. Slowly and with more reluctance than she wanted to show, she pulled back and pressed her fingertips against his lips. "Be careful, Adam," she whispered hoarsely and with intense sincerity. "It would be very ungallant of you to break my heart."

A flicker of surprise and possibilities lit the golden flecks in his eyes. "And most unprofessional, Katie, for you to break mine."

The surprise moved from his eyes to hers and she had an impulse to laugh at the unlikely idea that either of them were in such danger. But laughter was beyond her capability just then and would have been much akin to tempting fate. "I guess we can both consider ourselves warned then, can't we?" With a smile that trembled uncertainly on her lips, she picked up the picnic basket, ready to share the burden of carrying it. "I'm hungry," she said, resolutely cheerful. "How long until we eat?"

SEDUCTION WAS NOT part of Adam's original plan. He'd thought a few hours together ought to do the trick. Dinner, maybe a walk on the beach. Time to delve a bit into Katie's background, discover perhaps why she intrigued him so, send a clear signal to his brothers that he wasn't just jealous, he was staking a definite claim. No veiled warnings, no count-me-in as a competitor. Until the party was past, until Katie had accomplished the job he'd brought her here to do, Adam intended to let Bryce—and Peter, too, if he had any thoughts of courting Katie in earnest—know that she was not available. He meant to cut his brothers out and himself in with one carefully planned, strategic evening.

He'd been patting himself on the back ever since the idea of the picnic had occurred to him. It was a touch of brilliance, he thought. A real *Katie* kind of date, with its air of spontaneity and intimacy, fun and clandestine romance. She could go barefoot if she wanted. In fact, he half-hoped she would. The funny part of the whole idea was how much he'd antici-pated the moment she'd open the door and see him there with a picnic basket. He'd found random smiles sneaking up on him all day, even during the rather serious contract meeting with his team and Wallace's attorneys. It could have been embarrassing if he hadn't kept a glass of water handy as a tool to hide his inappropriate glee.

It hadn't once occurred to him throughout the long day that Katie might not agree to go with him. Nor had he spent a single minute worrying that she might honestly prefer Bryce's company to his. He'd planned a picnic and she would want to go. It was as simple as that.

Until the moment she opened the door and the questions floored him with a sudden and unsettling nervousness. She was wearing the red dress again, this time with a slender silver chain around her neck and a tiny puff-heart pendant nestled at the hollow of her throat. Her hair curled in subdued ringlets around her face and he'd never, in his life, seen eyes so blue. A man could drown in those eyes...and never once struggle for air. What if she wouldn't go with him? What if she said a resounding, no?

But she seemed thunderstruck to see him at her door and from there, the whole thing had gone pretty much as he'd planned. Right up until the moment in the hall when she kissed him and told him not to break her heart. From that point on, he was a drowning man, certain that seduction had been in the back of his mind all along. He just didn't know if it had been in his plan or hers, or was the unexpected result of the two converging. Whatever the cause, he suddenly could think of nothing except the effect, which was the impulsive desire to kiss her until she couldn't breathe, to caress her and stroke her, and tease her into begging him to make love to her. He wanted that suddenly more than he'd wanted anything in a very long time.

He'd planned to drive down to Watch Hill Cove for the picnic. He'd asked Benson earlier to pull out the little BMW convertible he drove for fun and put the top down. Somehow a bit of speed, that cruising-low-to-the-ground rush, a touch of daring seemed the right mood to set for the evening he had in mind. But before they'd made it even halfway to the garage, Katie set about changing his plans. "Why should we drive all the way to the beach when there's a perfect picnic spot right here?"

He couldn't think where she meant. "Here?"

"The gardens," she said, gesturing toward the grounds. "You have this wonderful, exotic display of nature right here at Braddock Hall." She tipped her head to the side. "And I'll bet you haven't been inside the solarium in years."

"I was there only a couple of months ago," he said in self-defense, although he'd only stepped in at his Grandfather's bidding to see some new fern recently imported from South America. "And the beach should be very nice by the time we get there. Not too hot. Not too crowded."

"But not as private as the spot I have in mind."

Now, why would any man in his right mind argue with that?

Chapter Eight

Adam picnicked the way he did everything else…efficiently, focused and with a cell phone clipped to his side. Before they even reached the end of the hall, Katie had realized this was a man with a *plan.* And the obvious thing to do, if she wanted to throw him off-balance, which she did, was to set out to change those plans. So she suggested the solar-ium…and wondered the moment they were deep within its damp, exotic greenness if an invitation into her bedroom would have been any more blatant. In an hour, surely no longer than that, the glass dome over their heads would reflect the shining of a million stars and the golden glow of a nearly full moon. Around the spot where Adam had spread out the quilt, plants with large, thick leaves vied to provide privacy for the picnic. Katie had been in the solarium with Archer practically every afternoon since her ar-rival, but it had never before had such an intimate *feel,* such a primitive jungle wildness. *Let's get it on* might just as well have been flashing in green neon lights right above her curly head.

She, who had imagined being this alone with

Adam a few dozen times, hadn't expected to be struck with nerves the moment it happened. But she was so antsy she had trouble sitting still on her side of the quilt. She was too restless and excited to eat more than a few bites of the meal Abbott had so painstakingly packed. She had too many butterflies in her stomach to allow the champagne to work its magic. She was too unsure of what would happen next to relax. Would Adam kiss her? Did he need some encouragement? Should she pour him some more champagne? Would it be smarter to put her common sense into action and run as far away and as fast as she could? Or should she just call him on his cell phone and tell him she'd like to try out a few fantasies with him?

"So you were raised by grandparents, too." He continued talking, making conversation as if the air wasn't charged with an electric attraction, as if they weren't sequestered in a lovely, deep green solitude, as if the champagne wasn't bubbling in their glasses, catching and reflecting the light of the tall, tapered, elegant candles. Abbott, it turned out, knew something about the esthetics necessary for a romantic picnic.

"Yes," Katie answered. Her throat felt dry and scratchy. So she coated it with more champagne.

His smile came slowly and with gentle chiding. "I've told you at least a dozen stories about my growing up in the past thirty minutes and you've answered every one of my questions with a sketchy yes or no. Are you being deliberately mysterious, Katie?"

"I didn't think I should talk with my mouth full."

She licked her fingers to lend credence to the idea she'd been too busy eating to talk. "Abbott packs a mean picnic basket."

"He's had a great deal of practice over the years. My Grandmother Jane loved summer picnics."

"And indoor camp-outs," she said to show she remembered.

"Those, too." Adam folded his napkin, ran his fingers down the crease. "I'd still like to hear about your childhood. As we were both raised by grandparents, I think it gives us some basic experiences in common."

Katie sighed. She didn't like to remember those times, even though she'd promised herself she would never forget them, either. "Living with my grandparents wasn't a particularly happy arrangement for any of us. My father and I went to live with them when I was six, only a couple of months after my mother died and then...he died, too, a couple of months later. After that, it was just my grandparents and me."

"No aunts, uncles, cousins?"

"No. Just the three of us."

He frowned. "Were you...mistreated?"

She let her lips form a half smile. "They didn't beat me or anything like that. I was just more responsibility than they wanted to have at that time in their lives. And they really missed my dad."

"As if you didn't?" He said it with an edgy disgust.

"They were as good to me as they knew how to be. And in their way, I think they loved me." She cleansed the memory with a wry little smile. "Don't get me wrong, Adam. I'm grateful for every minute of the life I've had and they had a big influence on that. For the better. I only wish they could have known more happiness themselves.''

''They're no longer living?''

She shook her head, wishing she felt more than a vague regret at their absence from her life. ''They died within a year of each other. Very soon after I left their house for the last time.''

''How old were you then?''

''When I finally marshaled enough courage to go, you mean? Seventeen. Barely.''

His eyebrows went up. Lying on his side, as he was, propped easily on his arm, Adam looked relaxed, interested and totally focused. On her. And what she was saying. ''I left home for college at sixteen,'' he said. ''I've never been so terrified in my life…or so determined not to let it show.''

She folded her napkin, too, and ran the crease through her fingers. ''Leaving my grandparents' house was what I wanted more than anything else,'' she said. ''I'd planned it for years…and it was still the scariest thing I've ever done.''

His smile was understanding, and the ensuing moment of quiet was more companionable than any she had ever known. ''Where did you go?'' he asked after a while.

She shrugged. ''Everywhere. Anywhere. I spent most of my growing up years looking at maps and reading books about other places. So when I left Oklahoma, it was just a matter of searching out some of those places.''

''It can't have been that simple.''

"Not at first, maybe. But my favorite game as a child was to close my eyes, spin around three times, and jab my finger at a map. Whatever town was closest to the end of my finger was the *winner*." She smiled, remembering the great pleasure of discovery. "Then I imagined living there and what kind of life I'd have in the place I imagined it to be."

"Sounds a little lonely."

"I lost my whole life before I turned seven. Loneliness just sort of came with the territory." She hadn't said that to anyone else. Ever. But, somehow, she felt Adam understood, even before the words were spoken. "You lost your mother at an early age," she said to draw him out and to stop talking about her own childhood. "You must know what I mean."

He started to deny it, but then...he didn't. "For a long time, I believed my mother died rather than take on the responsibility of raising me. I thought there must be something really wrong with me. It doesn't make sense now, of course, but then...well, I was a child and both of my parents had abandoned me and I thought it had to be my fault, somehow."

"Your father?" Katie asked the question softly, not liking to intrude, but she genuinely liked James and she wanted to understand how his life choices had affected Adam's. "He wasn't around much when you were a child?"

"He made the occasional stab at fatherhood, but he was never very successful at it." Adam turned the cloth napkin over and traced the crease on the opposite side. "My grandmother said he loved my mother so much that something in him died with her and he got lost in the search to find his heart again. Most of the time, I can believe that.'' He shrugged. ''Then he'll show up with a little alley cat of a fiancée like Monica and I go back to thinking he never had a heart to lose.''

''But you had your grandparents to give you a good foundation and more love than most people ever know. You were lucky, Adam.''

''You're right.'' His smile conceded her point. ''I'm sorry you couldn't have been as fortunate.''

''Don't be,'' she said and meant it. ''My childhood sounds sordid and tragic when I talk about it, depressing even, but it wasn't. Who knows? If my parents had survived and given me a home, I might have turned out to be a rebellious punk with pink hair, multiple body piercings and a really bad attitude.''

He laughed. ''When you put it like that, I'm glad you only wound up with a ring on your toe.''

She felt a little thrill that he had, at least, noticed her foot jewelry and decided that for the party she would paint her toenails in ten different circus colors. ''Your grandfather likes my ring,'' she said. ''I'm thinking of getting him one for his birthday.''

Adam laughed again, with real humor. ''I'm sure he'd be very appreciative. He seems to think anything you do is pretty spectacular. I don't know how you managed to bewitch him so completely.''

Katie felt a pang of disappointment that Adam, apparently, didn't find her accomplishments quite so *spectacular*. Obviously, she hadn't managed to bewitch *him*. ''I adore your grandfather,'' she said. ''He's a really wonderful man.''

"You'd have liked Grandmother, too. And she, I'm certain, would have liked you."

"I'm sure she and I would have gotten along splendidly. The way your grandfather talks about her, she was a very special lady." Katie put the champagne flute to her lips and let the last drops dribble onto her tongue. "I certainly like her grandsons."

He smoothly reached up and took the glass from her hand, setting it aside, and turning the air into a sudden, steamy current of sexuality. "All of them?" he asked. "Equally?"

She ran the tip of her tongue across her lips, tasting the lingering effervescence of the champagne. "It would be rude and impolite of me to name a favorite, don't you think? I am, after all, a guest."

"Hmm." His fingertips brushed across the top of her hand, sending a fiery shiver of anticipation rocketing up her arm. "I suppose that might depend on whose guest you are."

She knew where this was leading, and she meant to follow it through to its inevitable conclusion, but one of them was going to have to be more direct. No reason it shouldn't be her. "Are we talking about whose house I'm a guest in...or whose bedroom?"

For a second, he looked startled, then amusement tucked in at the corners of his mouth. "Have you been a guest in a bedroom other than your own?"

"Well, not lately," she said, wishing she could tell a bald-faced lie to wipe the confident look off his handsome visage. But lying took so much energy and it rarely turned out to be fun. "Not that it's any of your business."

"You're right. And if it had happened in my

house, I would have heard about it." He smiled with conviction. "It's a big house, but a small family."

She moistened her lips and decided to skip from direct to perfectly frank. "So, Adam, were you just curious to know if I'm sleeping with someone or are you working your way around to inviting me into your bed with you?"

His eyebrows arched, but only a little. "That's a direct question," he said softly. "And I believe it deserves a direct answer."

Katie couldn't have moved then if her life depended on it. She sat, her legs tucked to one side, one bare foot hooked in a fold of the quilt, her arms trembling for want of support, as he rose to his knees before her and cupped her face in his hands. For long, breathless seconds, he held her captive with no more than the desire in his whiskey-brown eyes. Her heart had stopped at his words and now waited for permission to beat again. His answer, when at last it came, was a kiss. Not like the first one. Nor like the second. This was no impulsive act. No surprise attack. His lips came to hers in the kind of long, slow, wet kiss Katie would have liked to linger in for days. Years, maybe. A kiss that had depth and possibly consequences, but she put all her energy into being present in the moment and enjoying every second of it.

Almost instantly, however, the attraction sprang from embers to flames inside her, pooling in a liquid rush of wanting and sending her arms around him, turning her live-in-the-moment philosophy into a pulsing need for the future. A future in which he would be naked. When she would be, too. When their bodies and hearts would come together in a thousand moments, each better and more intense than the last. She wanted him with an astoundingly complicated, and yet simple, desire. She wanted him to feel the same desperate, out-of-control passion already kindling within her.

But the firm, compelling pressure of his lips on hers, the steady grip of his hands on her shoulders, told her that the night ahead was planned out, already framed in soft, warm touches and a deliberately gradual escalation of ardor. He was in charge of himself, his emotions and her. It wasn't fair. It wasn't healthy. And she was suddenly positive she had to do something about it. Adam needed to lose control. He needed someone to show him how.

No reason it shouldn't be her.

ADAM THOUGHT IT OUT as he and Katie ate their picnic, weighing the pros and cons of taking this relationship into intimate territory. He kept the conversation moving, tried to get her to talk, but didn't press her. She picked at what food she took—he doubted she even knew what she was eating—and stuffed a considerable amount of it back in the basket when she thought he wasn't looking. Katie was nervous. A result, he was sure, of the sexual tension humming around them like an orchestra tuning up for the big night. He was a little nervous himself. Though it was more anticipation than anything else. But the lovemaking to come was a settled thing in his mind. Had been since the moment she'd kissed him. It was just a matter of waiting for the right time to suggest they return to the Hall and adjourn to his

bedroom. Her attack of nerves was endearing somehow, and made him feel tender and protective and
yes, *loving* toward her.

But he didn't want to rush. Katie was special, different from other women, a little on the shy side, a
lot unsophisticated, and he wanted to take extra time
to romance her, to put her at ease with him. Still, he
was surprised by her candid question, the invitation
she issued with such cool, and yet nervous, daring.
He liked her directness, appreciated the lack of social
game-playing. That was not often, if ever, a part of
his experience…whether he ended up inviting a
woman into his bed or not.

When he kissed her, he meant for it to be a vali-
dation, the seal of approval on and a gentle precursor
for the lovemaking to come. But he was totally un-
prepared for the rush of passion that flooded through
him like a high tide at the first touch of her lips, and
he had to fight down the sensation of drowning in
the sweet, heady taste of her. He felt a little dizzy,
in fact, and when she nudged him—pushed him, really—he allowed her to coerce him onto his back on
the quilt, wondering what she had in mind. The floor
was marbled stone and hard beneath him, despite the
slight cushioning of the padded quilt, but he hardly
noticed as she followed him down, her lips trailing
sensual kisses along his jaw, her hands whispering
across his chest.

He thought perhaps he'd suggest the bedroom
sooner than anticipated and he smiled a bit at the
idea that he'd worried about rushing her. Then she
nipped his ear…and lathed it with her tongue. Something happened to his lungs and his pulse jumped to

attention…as did other parts of his body. But before he could rouse enough energy to ask her what, exactly, she thought she was doing, her lips returned to his, smothering him in a kiss that was hard and hot, deep and demanding. Adam didn't think he'd ever been kissed with such explicit abandon and he knew for certain he'd never been so close to making love to a woman at the wrong time, in the wrong place.

He moved his arms to halt her impetuous rush into passion and, to his own amazement, found himself folding her into a crushing embrace, drawing her body quickly, insistently down to his. She stopped then, pulling back slightly to look into his eyes, smiling—*smiling!*—a sweet, satisfied little smile. "Don't get overanxious, Adam," she said in a throaty, sexier-than-hell whisper. "This is only the beginning of what I promise you will always remember as a spectacularly exciting night."

He blinked and in that split second of confusion, lost control. Of her, of himself, of the situation. Her hands were at the placket of his shirt, her fingers slipping beneath the fabric, lifting, and then he felt the jerk as she tried to rip off the buttons. They held fast and he couldn't help but be amused by her sigh of frustration. "Honestly, Adam," she said, sitting back on her heels. "aren't you uncomfortable wearing all this starch?"

"It's not starch," he said, reaching up to undo the buttons himself. "Just a very good fabric."

"I knew there was a reason I prefer cheap cotton." She tugged the shirttails free of his waistband with a flattering urgency. He let her wrestle the shirt open, and watched her frown when she saw his undershirt.

"I'm thinking a lesser woman would admit defeat at this point," she said.

"But you're *not* a lesser woman." It was as much hope as statement of fact.

"No, I'm not." She pulled at the undershirt, sending a spinning thrill cavorting across his skin. "Which is exceedingly lucky for you."

This he realized, was fun. Unfortunately, not the best place to get naked. "We can go back to the house," he suggested, not particularly crazy about the idea, but knowing it would be better now than a few minutes from now. "My bedroom will be a little more conducive to comfort."

Her concentration switched from his undershirt to his face. "This isn't about comfort, Adam. Haven't you ever been seduced before?"

Five minutes ago, he would have said an uncompromising yes, but now...well, now he wasn't so sure. "I think I'm about to find out I haven't," he said, his voice sounding rough and unsteady even in his own ears.

"When you're certain of it, let me know." She bent her head to his chest and pushing his undershirt out of her way, she blazed a trail of fire across his stomach with her lips and tongue...and moved lower, her hand slipping inside the waistband of his trousers. Adam had been with aggressive women before, but had always been aware throughout that his wealth and position was as much the object of their desire as his pleasure. Something was always expected from him in return. But Katie seemed to want nothing except for him to lie back and let her share the responsibility for making their pleasure a mutual decision.

He thought she honestly would have preferred it if he'd been wearing cheap cotton and she could have ripped it to shreds in the heat of her wildcat passion.

When his cell phone interrupted with an unnerving trill, he was annoyed but reached for it automatically. Katie got to it first, cut the power off in midring and tossed the phone behind her into a monstrosity of a fern. "Don't panic," she said. "I'm sure whoever it was will call again later."

"Whoever it was could come looking for us," he said, not caring at the moment if he ever received another phone call or even if the Mormon Tabernacle Choir showed up in the solarium.

Katie teased him with a long, slow slide of her fingertips across his chest. "Then they'll get an eyeful, won't they?" And she bent again to let her lips trail after her descending fingers.

He knew he should insist they go to his bedroom before this got any more serious. He was aware that anyone, at any time, could walk in on them here. Not likely, perhaps, but definitely possible. And he was surprised to realize the possibility lent a forbidden and frenzied sweetness to their kisses, a heightened excitement to every touch. Her every movement was intoxicating, and his passion was on the rise, sweeping him along with her on a strangely erotic and uncharted journey. When she pushed up onto her knees, caught the hem of the red dress, and shimmied it up and over her head, he knew it was too late to worry about whether they should or shouldn't be naked together in the solarium, whether or not they might get caught. She had really lovely breasts. He cupped them full and heavy in his hands and then leaned up to take one rosy, willing tip into his mouth. He realized she had stolen his illusion of control, wiped it out with her uninhibited desire, was seducing him with his own passion, and seemed to be having a wonderful time of it, too.

But he didn't want her to remember him as a lover who simply waited for her to give him pleasure, so he borrowed some of her tactics and rolled her over onto her back, providing himself with yet another delightful view and the opportunity to explore her body as she had just been exploring his. His mouth found the smooth hollows of her waist and from there, he lost track of time and space, of her machinations to get him out of the rest of his clothes, and of his collusion, in turn, to relieve her of the scrappy bit of silk that was the only thing, other than the dress, she'd been wearing. On some level, he noticed the delightful symmetry as their bodies blended into one and he noted by touch, and with a quickly distracted curiosity, the scarring on her lower back that gave her skin a dappled, silky texture beneath his hands.

But talking by that point was out of the question. Nothing made sense to him, except that she somehow reached past years of self-control and inner isolation to free emotions he hadn't known he possessed. She was wildly tender—very demanding—and he reciprocated in kind, touch for touch, kiss for kiss, pleasure for pleasure. She wanted his response, his attention, his total concentration and she would not settle for less. Luckily, neither would he. She had bewitched him until he couldn't even think about anything except her. As the night stretched into long conversations and endless possibilities, including, but not limited to, a canvas hammock, a chaise in a secluded corner of the garden, and not one, not two, but three different *campsites* in the north ell of the house, he forgot completely his original plan to end the evening in his own bed.

ADAM CAUGHT a yawn at breakfast and stifled it by lifting his coffee cup to his lips, but not, unfortunately, quickly enough to escape notice.

Bryce narrowed his gaze over a piece of whole wheat toast. "Did you stay up too late last night, big brother?"

"Yes," Adam answered, his expression carefully noncommittal, his tone warily neutral while under the table, Katie's bare foot slipped inside his pants leg and playfully massaged his calf.

"You look rough," Bryce continued cheerfully. "What were you doing all night? Watching the Tokyo markets instead of getting your quota of beauty rest?" He put the toast to his mouth, then lowered it without taking a bite as his curious gaze swung to Katie, seated next to Adam at the long cherry wood table. "Now, Katie, on the other hand, must have gotten a good night's sleep because she looks as perky as the Energizer Bunny this morning. But a whole lot cuter."

She smiled her thanks for the compliment and nibbled at a spiral slice of orange. "I had a very good night," she said. "Spectacular dreams."

"Adam must have brought you home early then." Bryce smiled from one to the other over his toast.

"Because I don't see any Japanese yen marks inked across your forehead."

"That's because he wrote them on my stomach," she said with a smile.

Adam choked on his coffee and her toes nipped his ankle.

Bryce stopped eating, a considering smile easing into his expression. "Don't tell me my brother has some imagination after all. You'll spoil my image of him."

"In that case, you definitely shouldn't look at his stomach." Katie's smile gave away the whole show and Adam, not knowing where to look, burned his tongue with a hasty gulp of coffee.

Bryce laughed, apparently more delighted by this information than jealous of it. "The things a guy will do to get back his tie. I'd intended to keep it because it goes so well with my yellow shirt, but...a deal's a deal."

Katie's toes stopped their clandestine nip and massage. "You made a bet with him?" she asked Adam, point-blank. "About last night?"

"He didn't mention that?" Bryce made a clucking noise with his tongue. "Now *that's* the big brother I know and love."

"There was no bet," Adam said quietly, but forcefully, gripping his fork too tightly. "And we'll talk about this later."

Katie frowned, while Bryce looked from one to the other, then happily attacked his eggs, glad to have stirred up some trouble, which most likely had been his only aim all along.

"I've invited a guest to join us for a few days

before the party,'' Archer announced abruptly, either oblivious to or deciding it would be politic to interrupt the conversation at the other end of the table. ''She'll arrive Sunday and stay through the week.''

''She?'' James entered the room in time to hear Archer's statement. Monica never appeared until sometime after eleven, as she was more night owl than morning glory, a fact which conspired to make breakfast a happier occasion for everyone. James seemed especially cheerful this morning and smiled pleasantly around the table as he pulled out a chair and joined the breakfast already in progress. ''So Dad, are you telling us you're bringing a *lady friend* out for the party?''

Archer glanced up, his gaze narrowing at the insinuation. ''I wouldn't think you'd object, James, as you are constantly bringing *your* lady friends home with you.''

James's cheerful mood faded. ''Of course, I have no objection, Dad. This is your house and it is your birthday party. I was merely wondering if this is someone special…someone, perhaps, we should all get to know.''

Adam reached for his coffee cup again, aware of the tension bristling between his father and grandfather, between himself and Bryce, even wafting his way from Katie, who'd become suddenly and uncharacteristically engrossed in the food she was not eating.

''Yes, James,'' Archer said. ''She is a special friend. A very special friend. Someone you certainly should make the effort to know. Perhaps you remember her…Ilsa Fairchild?''

James looked as if someone had just kicked him in the shin. "Ilsa?" he repeated, his voice stumbling over the dual syllables.

"You may recall her husband, Ian, too," Archer continued. "I believe you and he were at Harvard about the same time."

"Ilsa?" James repeated the name again as if he couldn't believe he'd gotten it correctly the first time.

Smiling now, Archer cut into his poached egg. "She never remarried, you know, after Ian died."

"I didn't know." James picked up his coffee cup, set it down without taking a drink. "She's...coming here, to Braddock Hall?"

"That's right. I invited her...as my special guest." Archer nodded in a way that defied anyone to challenge him. "As you said, it is my birthday party."

"But, Dad...she's *my* age."

Archer paused, a chunk of egg white poised on the end of his fork. "And your fiancée is no older than Bryce. I fail to see how age is relevant to this conversation."

The remainder of Adam's appetite slunk away. So much for a hearty breakfast, he thought. Beside him, he felt Katie's tension, and across the table, he could see his brother's apprehension etched into his carefully careless expression. Now, however, the focus had shifted to the other end of the table and the incredible possibility that Archer was romantically involved with Ilsa Fairchild.

James twisted his cup in its saucer. "How...how did you become acquainted with...with Ilsa?"

"She and your mother worked together on the library board. I've run into her a few times since. She's a lovely woman.''

''Y-yes, she was always very…attractive.'' James shook his head, as if he were trying to clear it of misconceptions. ''The last I heard she was starting a business. Something unusual, like making match—''

''Connections,'' Archer supplied without missing a beat. ''She has a small public relations firm. IF Enterprises.''

''I've had lunch with her,'' Adam said, in an attempt to signal James that this was…must be, in fact…a serious attachment.

''So have I.'' Bryce exchanged a meaningful look with Adam and for a moment, they shared the bonding of apprehension. It wasn't that they didn't want Archer to be happy, of course, but the idea of any woman coming into the position their Grandmother Jane had occupied so completely was startling at best.

''Yes,'' Archer agreed cheerily. ''And I arranged for Peter to meet her, too.''

James, looking uncomfortable with this information, glanced at the uniformed maid, who immediately filled his glass with fresh-squeezed juice. ''Ilsa Fairchild,'' he said almost to himself, as if he still couldn't quite believe it.

''She used to come into The Torrid Tomato every week for lunch,'' Katie said, her tone trying to bridge the gap between awkwardness and a less intense topic of conversation. ''I call her Mrs. If.''

An icy chill tumbled down Adam's spine to collide with the unsettling prospect of a new family crisis. His gaze narrowed on Katie's smiling face, the frame of dark curls around her face, her blue, blue eyes and suddenly he remembered where he'd seen her before. *The Torrid Tomato. His lunch with Ilsa. The laughing ballerina of a waitress.* "That was you," he said, stunned at the discovery, his voice accusing, thick with displeasure. "The *waitress.*"

Katie's smile vanished and the icy chill that had begun in him crystallized in her eyes.

"Mr. Adam?" Abbott appeared beside Adam's chair, drawing his attention momentarily away. "Frederick, one of the gardeners, brought this to the house just now. He found it in the solarium, in a potted plant there, and thought you had mislaid it." The butler placed Adam's cell phone next to his plate and backed away from the table.

"Thank you, Abbott." Adam picked up the small phone and, noted with disgust, that his hand was shaking. Trying to gain control of a sudden, heart-deep feeling of betrayal, he used the corner of his napkin to wipe off a speck of dirt and then dropped the phone into his pocket. "Thank Frederick, too, please."

"Yes, Mr. Adam."

"You left your phone in the solarium?" Bryce's eyebrows were up, his gaze shifting from Adam to Katie and back again, sensing disaster, perhaps, but unsure of its source. "In a potted plant?"

"It appears so." There was no graceful way out of this, Adam realized as he tried to think of a reasonable explanation for Katie's deception. But the only alibi which occurred to him was that she was an opportunist and he had fallen, quite willingly, into her trap...just as his father did on a regular basis with each successive wife. Just as now, possibly, his grandfather was doing with the Fairchild woman.

Across the table, Bryce raised his glass to Katie in salute. "You separated Adam from his cell phone," he said. "I'm impressed, Ms. Canton. Deeply impressed."

"You should be," she replied, although her smile lacked conviction. "It was quite an accomplishment for a…waitress."

Adam took the hit, determined not to let her attitude derail his quite justified indignation. "You might have told me," he said, hating to believe she'd lied to him so thoroughly.

Her gaze narrowed. "About working as a waitress? Or as a bartender? Don't raise your eyebrows. They are both noble professions." Anger flared in her voice. "I've been a secretary, too. Also, a grocery-store checker, a photographer's assistant, and a dog groomer. I haven't taken a turn as an exotic dancer just yet, but that could be next. Do you find those occupations as objectionable or is it only serving food and drinks that bothers you?" She pushed her chair back. "Don't answer that. I believe you've made it very plain already."

"I think I deserve an explanation."

"Try not to be such an arrogant snob, Adam. Difficult as you may find it to believe, that could cause me to lose my good opinion of you. Excuse me, please." With a tight hold on her anger, she nodded to the others at the table, motioned them all to remain in their seats when they, belatedly, started to rise, and headed for the door.

Adam let out his breath, realizing only then he'd been holding it in.

"Katie," he said sternly, stopping her in the doorway, thinking he had to let her know he would not be lied to.

She whirled around, fury in every line of her slender body, hurt in the flash of her stormy blue eyes. "What is it, Adam? Did I forget something?" As she spoke, she picked up the nearest pitcher from the sideboard and approached the table. "A refill, perhaps?" She topped off his glass, filling it to the brim with water and ice so that he couldn't possibly pick it up without spilling. "Anything else?"

He was angry, too, now. She'd misinterpreted his remark, was acting childishly. As if *she* were the injured party here. "You should have been honest with me from the beginning."

She stared at him for a minute, then dumped the remaining ice water in his lap. "And you, Adam, should learn to listen." Setting the crystal pitcher on the table with a heavy *thunk,* she spun on her heels and walked barefoot from the room, leaving a stunned and startled audience in her wake.

Chapter Nine

"I wish you could have been here to see the look on his face." Archer concluded his accounting of the morning's events, his voice at the other end of the phone line fairly blooming with satisfaction. "I don't imagine my grandson has ever been so befuddled by a woman in his life."

Ilsa thought it was more likely Adam had never been angrier in his life. Proud as he was—as all the Braddock men were—she couldn't imagine he'd be in a forgiving mood anytime soon. She sighed. Smaller things than a quart of ice water had ruined many a promising romance. "Did he say anything?"

"Not a word. Just brushed off the ice cubes, waved away the towel Abbott tried to foist on him and stalked from the room. He left for work a few minutes ago...in a different, dry suit and with his nose still considerably out of joint." Archer chuckled. "I'll tell you for a fact, Ilsa, I wasn't sure about Katie the first time I saw her, but I have new respect for your insights. She's possibly the only woman in the world who can keep my oldest grandson on his toes."

"As long as there's a pitcher of ice water around, I can't think it would be difficult."

Archer laughed in earnest, mistaking her dry comment for a joke. The truth was, Ilsa had very much hoped Katie and Adam were on a path to the genuine discovery of each other and the love of a lifetime, but she feared this incident would be a setback. She couldn't imagine Adam Braddock allowing anyone to treat him so. The embarrassment alone would be difficult for him to acknowledge, much less any justification for the action. In her heart, she was proud of Katie for standing up to him, even if she was disappointed at this unforeseen turn of events. "Is that all that happened?" she asked, wanting to make sure Archer hadn't left out some small, but important detail.

"Well, they all think you and I are an *item*."

"What?"

"They think you're my special *lady friend*."

Ilsa was completely taken aback by that bit of left-over information. "You mean they believe we're *more* than friends?"

"James jumped to that conclusion the minute I mentioned I'd invited you to be a houseguest. Adam and Bryce followed his lead like puppies and I have no doubt one or both of them have already had Peter on the phone to bring him up to speed on the situation." He chuckled with a hearty enjoyment. "I've been having a good laugh about it with Janey this morning." His voice turned wistful. "I'm only wishing, of course, but if she were here, I know she'd be enjoying this even more than I am."

Listening to him, Ilsa couldn't imagine how anyone, especially his son and grandsons, could think another woman would ever claim a significant place in his heart. "I can't believe James was serious," she said and recognized the question unintentionally tucked into her voice. "He was probably only teasing you."

"He may have started out that way, but you should have seen his face when I told him your name. If he didn't before, he certainly left the breakfast table mortally afraid that you and I are romantically involved. And don't go thinking I said anything to warrant such an assumption, because I merely stated the facts…leaving out the real reason you and I have formed our little alliance, of course. My son was pretty shaken up by what he imagines is going on, too, and I think it has a lot more to do with you than because he's worried about somebody stepping into his mother's place."

Ilsa could read between the lines well enough to know Archer had decided to try a bit of matchmaking himself. Although she didn't like the idea that he was dangling her in front of James like a prize to be won, she recognized the swift kick of a thrill, too. And she liked that even less. "If you're going to play matchmaker, Archer, you should be aware there can be serious consequences. James is engaged to be married and not interested in me other than as an old acquaintance."

"In a few days, Ilsa, I'll have lived a full seventy-nine years and I'm not about to spend a minute of the life I have left worrying about consequences. James makes a fool of himself without my assistance on a regular basis. Don't begrudge me the opportunity to help him do it just this once.''

''I'm looking forward to meeting his fiancée,'' Ilsa said to clarify her position, despite her rather rebellious emotions. ''I'm sure she's delightful.''

''Delightful isn't the way I'd describe Monica, but you go ahead and look forward to meeting her. Anticipation, in this case, has reality beat to a standstill.''

Deciding it was futile to argue, Ilsa returned to the original purpose for his call. ''What do you think Adam will do, once he's cooled off?''

''No pun intended?'' Archer's humor faded to a more serious note. ''He'll fire her. No doubt about it. I won't let him, of course. I'll hit him with all the practical reasons it's not feasible to change coordinators at this late date, then I'll persuade her it's her duty to stay and see the party through to the end. She's not a quitter and well, she likes me nearly as much as I like her. I think she'd genuinely hate to miss my birthday.''

Yes. That was Ilsa's feeling, too. But at this point it was hard to know how far the relationship had progressed or if it could weather this first bout of disenchantment. The main thing she wanted, now, was to persuade Archer not to interfere. ''Not every match turns out the way I'd like, Archer. You should be careful not to alienate your grandson in your desire to make this one work.''

''Pshaw,'' he scoffed with a touch of the Braddock arrogance.

''All I'm saying is that it might be wise to stand back just now.'' She offered the advice with little hope of his following it. "Let Adam and Katie learn to follow their hearts in their own way."

"Hands off, you mean."

She gentled her voice, hoping he'd take her words to heart. "It is, if you'll recall, Archer, one of my stipulations."

"If you could have seen his face, Ilsa…. He's fallen as hard and fast for her as I did for my Janey. Adam is in love, probably for the first and last time in his life. I recognize the signs, even if he doesn't."

"Then you only need to let him realize that for himself."

He sighed. "There's always a catch, isn't there?"

Her lips found a smile. "You knew in the beginning this wasn't going to be easy."

"Yes," he said. "Are you sure you can't come before Sunday?"

"That's only a couple of days away and it'll take me that long to think about this situation and figure out how—and *if*—I can stir up the possibilities again. Let's be still and see what develops between now and then."

His gruff chuckle was resigned, but confident. "And that's exactly what Janey would say."

"I'll see you on Sunday and, in the meantime, please try to avoid the temptation to act as matchmaker."

"For Adam and Katie? Or for James and…you?"

"Both," she said, more sharply than she'd intended.

But his laughter as he bade her goodbye was far from reassuring.

"I want to see Lara in my office," Adam said as he passed Nell's desk without slowing his agitated stride one iota.

"Now?" Nell called after him, clearly alarmed by his mood.

"No," he snapped, out of patience with the world. "Five minutes ago." He tossed his briefcase onto his desk and strode to the window, growing angrier by the second. Damn females. All of them. Everywhere. They'd all been put on earth just to aggravate him. *Learn to listen.* As if they made any sense to begin with. As if they could make a point without resorting to dumping a pitcher of ice water in a man's lap. He could still feel the chilly humiliation, more than an hour later. And to accuse him of being a snob. *Him!* She was the one in need of lessons on how to treat another person with respect. She was the one who needed to learn to listen. She was the one who...

"You wanted to see me?"

Lara's voice from the doorway was solid, no-nonsense, and openly curious. He didn't bother to turn around, mainly because he knew she'd read something into his expression that wasn't there. "How quickly can you get a background check done?"

"Depends who it is and what you want to know."

"Background," he said sharply. "A personal history from age zero to...well, to whatever it is now. Family, education, jobs, friends, previous relationships...everything."

Lara, being Lara, picked up on his one slip of the tongue. "*Previous* relationships?"

"That's what I said, isn't it?" He couldn't remember the last time he'd been so angry, so completely furious with another person—Katie, of course—or so upset at the way he was handling his emotions. Or not handling them. "I want a dossier on Kate Canton on my desk before the ink has time to dry on the paper."

"Okay." Lara's tone was hesitant and just on the safe side of amused. "She's the party planner you hired, isn't she?"

"She is. Any other *pertinent* questions?"

"I believe that is considered pertinent, Adam. Occupation is a good place to start when researching someone's life."

"In that case, you should look up waitresses, too." He felt a pang at saying it that way, as if he was upset because of what she did for a living. And he wasn't. He was upset because she'd lied to him about it.

"She worked as a waitress?" Lara was already enjoying his misery a little too much. He could tell by her voice.

"There's nothing wrong with that," he said, turning. "It's a noble profession."

She didn't even try to conceal her smile. *"Noble?"*

"It's an honest way to make a living," he snapped. "Do you have something against waiters and waitresses?"

"Oh, no. I've done my time waiting tables and made some good money doing it." She paused, trying to assess his strange mood. "But I never thought of it as particularly *noble*."

"You're wasting my time, Lara. I want that information."

"I'll call Nelson. If she's been anywhere on the Internet, he'll have her profiled in a matter of minutes."

Adam frowned. "I wouldn't count on it being that easy." With a touch of his hand, he buzzed Nell. "Get me the occupancy projections for the Boston office building." He'd switched off, before he belatedly remembered to punch in her intercom number again and offer a conciliatory, "Please."

Lara was still in the doorway, curiosity etched all over her lovely face, but at his glance, she turned to go.

"Lara," he stopped her. "While you're at it, find out what you can about Ilsa Fairchild, too."

Her carefully arched eyebrows lifted. "Kate Canton. Ilsa Fairchild," she repeated as if etching the names in her memory. But what she was really after was his reasons for wanting the information. He knew it, and she knew that he knew. "Hmm. Two women whose names have been floating around this office lately like rumors. What *are* you up to, Adam?"

For a moment, he thought about confiding in her. But only for a moment. "Six foot four and still growing," he said. "Now get out of my office and prove you're worth the exorbitant salary I pay you."

"And then some," she said and closed the door behind her. She opened it again almost before it latched. "Do you have a social security number?"

"I thought you'd have that memorized. You probably have occasion to refer to it more than I do."

"Not *your* social security number, Adam. It would be helpful, although not strictly necessary, to have one for the women you want investigated."

Investigated. The word sounded so invasive, so not what he wanted to do. But he had to know. The safety of his family was his responsibility. "I don't know," he said, picking up a report off his desk. "Ask Nell if she has it. She wrote out the retainer check for Katie…and who knows how many thousands of dollars more for the party." The thought that he'd trusted Katie so completely was amazing to him suddenly. It had never once occurred to him to question her. He'd been so determined she would work for him, he hadn't even taken basic precautions. He'd instructed Nell in the beginning to give Katie anything she asked for and now his stomach knotted in disappointment that she might have, probably had, done much more than lie to him. He'd certainly given her the perfect opportunity. "I doubt Nell will have Mrs. Fairchild's social security number, but it amazes me sometimes what she has in that computer."

"I'll check with her." Lara closed the door again, but was back within a few minutes to hand him the occupancy projections and a bit of information. "No retainer," she told him crisply.

"What?" He looked up from the report he hadn't been reading.

"Your events coordinator hasn't requested so much as a cough drop."

That was odd. But his black mood lightened instantly to a cautious gray. "I distinctly remember telling her to call Nell and arrange to pick up a check.''

Lara shrugged. "She never called. Unless someone else has been paying her, she hasn't received a single dime to date."

He frowned. "Nothing for caterers, supplies for the party?"

"Not through Nell."

But *through Nell* was about the only way his money was ever disbursed. He used cash and credit cards, but Nell paid the bills. At home, it worked much the same, with expenditures handled mainly by Ruth or Abbott, subject to either his or his grandfather's okay.

"I'll have to check on that," he said, although he couldn't fathom who he might check with. He would have known if the money was tapped from the household accounts. His grandfather wouldn't expect to carry the cost of his own birthday party and would have questioned Adam about any request for funds. Certainly James wouldn't volunteer to pay, and it wouldn't occur to either Bryce or Peter that their older brother didn't have the monetary issues all under control. So unless Nell had made a mistake, which was highly unlikely, Katie hadn't been paid. Hadn't, in fact, asked to be paid.

Lara left again and Adam let the report drop back onto his desk. Turning to the broad expanse of window, he gazed unseeingly out at the river and the sure signs that spring was fading into summer. He should, he supposed, be wondering if Katie had made any preparations at all for the party, if she'd lined up even the most basic resources needed to put together an event worthy of being called a Braddock party. But he wasn't truly concerned about that part. Bryce had said she was working on it and there were suppliers all over Rhode Island who were eager to work for his family. He couldn't imagine that even one of them would worry if they weren't paid in advance. It was Katie who occupied his thoughts. Katie, who hadn't even made a phone call to request the wage he'd agreed to pay her. Katie, who collected experiences instead of material things.

And just that quickly his anger was gone, replaced by a subtle and soothing relief. It was too soon, would be too impulsive to give up his suspicions entirely—plus he felt a little embarrassed that a lack of mercenary evidence could so quickly change his opinion. There were other things to consider, of course. But images of Katie, snippets of things she'd said were moving from the shadows of his mind, bringing with them a tender and tenacious longing, an emotion he couldn't quite name. Or perhaps wasn't ready to acknowledge.

He wasn't wholly ready to forgive her either. She had poured a pitcher of ice-cold water all over him only a couple of hours ago. He didn't believe he'd deserved that. Not even if he were an arrogant snob, which he wasn't. But she was, or had been, a waitress when he met her and she had no business going around passing herself off as an events coordinator. Maybe she and Ilsa Fairchild were in this ruse together.

Or maybe there was a perfectly logical explanation.

Turning back to the desk, Adam buzzed Nell.

"Hold my calls," he said when she answered. "And don't let anyone, not even Lara, come through that door."

"Whatever you say, Mr. Braddock."

Now there was a woman after his own heart, he thought. But as he settled into his big, leather chair, Katie was the only woman who seemed to have a claim on his heart. It was only of her that he thought. He recalled with soft delight how she had so easily turned Bryce's teasing back on him this morning, how she had been as quick as the Energizer Bunny to let anyone listening know she had spent a night possessed of spectacular dreams. Whether or not they realized she had spent the night with him was unimportant. He knew. And she knew. And that was spectacular enough.

He closed his eyes and recalled the sweetly sinful feel of her bare foot rubbing his leg under the table, out of view, but somehow erotically public. He let himself exult for just a minute in the feeling of satisfaction that she had chosen him over his brothers, and hadn't hesitated to say so.

Slowly, deliberately, he sank into the memories of last night, of Katie in the solarium, exerting a great deal of energy to seduce him, of her enthusiasm, of her body, naked and lovely in his arms. He let the images seep through him, vivid and intoxicating, until they took up all of his thoughts, all of his attention, and curved his lips into a soft smile of sheer and simple pleasure.

She was, he'd discovered, a woman of extremes. Fire in the night. Ice water in the morning. At the moment, that seemed a fair enough trade.

KATIE PACED from the leafy Boston fern to the dark green, feathery spikes of the Norfolk pine. "He'll probably never speak to me again."

Archer carefully patted down a mound of potting soil. "Never's a long time."

"I don't care one way or the other," she said, half to herself as she made the return trip to the fern. "He deserved it, you know. He really did."

There was no point in disagreeing with her. She'd been working herself up to this for the past hour, ever since Archer had persuaded her to help him with his plantings and prunings in the arboretum this morning. He thought it was healthy for her to vent her whole spiel of emotions and, personally, he thought pouring the ice water in Adam's lap had been a magnificent way to make her point. "You're right," he said. "My grandson does need to learn to listen."

"You bet he does. If he'd listened to me in the first place…" She let her vehemence fade to a frown. "What I don't understand is how you—probably the nicest man I've ever met—could have such a…a *starched shirt* for a grandson."

"Oh, he comes from a long line of starched shirts, Katie. I was much like Adam when I was younger. Probably would have been just as consumed by work as he is, if Janey hadn't come along to keep my priorities straight. My father was all starch, all business, all the time. On the day of his final and fatal heart attack, the stubborn old fool ignored the doctors, left the hospital, and went to the office. Adam is probably going to turn out just like him…unless someone special comes along to adjust his attitude."

Katie sighed. "No doubt someone that special

won't have to dump ice water in his lap to do it.''
She made another fern to tree loop. ''He's going to
fire me, you know.''

''I imagine he may be thinking about it.''

''Of course he is. He can't have a *waitress* under
his roof. That would upset the balance of his universe, turn his world on its ear, signal the final hours
of humanity and civilization as he knows it. He has
to fire me. It's the only way to salve his pride.''

''Well, perhaps not the *only* way.'' Archer thought
he should stand up for Adam, at least a little. ''He
might settle for an apology.''

''From whom? The glass blower? The city, for
supplying the water? The maid who put the pitcher
on the sideboard? Abbott, for not wrestling it out of
my hands?'' She paused to draw a breath. ''And just
in case you missed it, the list of people who might
possibly owe him an apology does not include me.''

Archer smiled to himself. She had spunk. He'd
hand her that. And she wasn't intimidated by Adam.
Or any Braddock, apparently. Another plus in her
favor. ''I suppose he could just have you banished.''

She frowned and resumed pacing. ''I guess that's
better than having me vanish. Although you might
want to advise him that any suspicious disappear-
ances will be thoroughly investigated by the UWA.''
She paused, looked at him with a livewire spark in
her eyes. ''That's the United Waitresses' Association, of which I am proud to be a member.''

He smiled, so she'd know he was on her side. ''I
don't think it's the idea of your being a waitress that
bothers him.''

''Well, of course it is. You heard him this morning. *That was you? The waitress?* He couldn't have sounded more appalled, if he'd tried.''

"Sure he could have, if he'd tried." Archer chuckled, hoping to pull her out of her grump.

But instead of brightening, her eyes flashed a belated capitulation. "I'm sorry, Mr. Braddock, for venting like that. You're his grandfather and the last person I should be ranting to about this. I should be in my room, haranguing Adam in private while I pack, instead of maligning him to you." She paused, frowned, looked unhappy, but resigned. "I wish I could be here for the party, but there's no way I can stay now. He's going to fire me and I'll have to leave. Probably today."

"I'm not going to let him fire you, Katie."

Her smile thanked him. "He's your grandson. It's more important that he be here, and happy, for your party than for me to stick around and cause problems. The arrangements are all set, basically. Someone else could oversee the final preparations. There's really no reason for you to stick your neck out for me."

Archer decided, despite Ilsa's cautionary advice, to run just a bit of interference. "Other than the fact that I want you to be at my birthday party?" he began gently. "Other than the fact that I hate to see my grandson throw away his best chance at true love because of a little ice water?"

Katie stopped pacing altogether. "T-true love?" she repeated, her voice squeaking on the words, as if he had made a joke and she hadn't quite caught the punchline.

Sending a silent apology to Ilsa, Archer plunged on. "I knew ten minutes after I met my Janey that I would love her until the day I died. It took about two weeks to convince her that I wasn't crazy and two years of marriage before she confessed it had taken her less than a minute to know I was the right guy for her. I'm telling you that, Katie, because love is a precious gift, whether it happens in an instant or grows slower than an oak tree. Adam has found that gift in you, Katie. He's in love with you. You must know that, even if he doesn't.''

Her expression shifted, all trace of humor blanching into panic. ''L-love?'' she repeated again. ''Oh, no, I don't think so. He hardly knows me. He doesn't even like me. He wants me to be different, not impulsive, more like him. He wants me to wear shoes.'' Her voice trailed off, but Archer could see the rundown of evidence as it flitted across her expression and then, the dawning of awareness in her eyes, the coalescence of possibility…probability…certainty— not that Adam was in love with her, but that she was in love with him. Truly. For always. She looked stunned, scared…and determined not to show it. ''No,'' she denied. ''We come from completely different backgrounds, have conflicting ideas about what's important. It would never work, even if…even if…'' But he could see the barriers falling even as she struggled to list them. ''I mean, he comes from all this. He's a Braddock.'' She gestured vaguely, encompassing the power, wealth and privilege that was a viable part of the name. ''And I'm a…a waitress!''

''Don't be a snob, Katie. You're a woman of many talents. He's a man with unplumbed depths. Adam shouldn't be punished because his last name is Braddock, any more than you should be penalized for who you have chosen to be. It's the experiences of your hearts you need to consider, not the separate lives you've led up until your paths merged onto this one." He could see he'd overdone it, pushed too hard. She was backing away from him in spirit, even before her feet took the first backward steps. Realizing he probably should have heeded Ilsa's advice, Archer touched her hand, leaving a streak of rich, dark soil on her fair skin. "Forgive an old man his meddling, Katie," he said. "I shouldn't have said anything. Mark it down to the sobering reality of yet another birthday. I had hoped to see at least one of my grandsons settled by now, had thought perhaps I might live to see the start of a new generation of Braddocks." He let his voice quaver a little, shamelessly appealing to her sympathy. "Age makes a man soft, you know, in the heart as well as the head...and I'm not embarrassed to say that if I could choose for Adam, you'd be my pick."

Her eyes misted with emotion. Or at least, Archer chose to believe they did. "Thank you," she said and leaned forward to press an affectionate kiss to his wizened cheek. "That's a lovely thing to say, but—"

He held up a hand to stop her. "I know. I should mind my own business."

"He's going to fire me," she said, as if it were certain.

"Stay for my party, Katie. Please."

She was reluctant to commit. "I'll stay until Adam orders me to go," she compromised.

When she had left and he was alone in the deep

green sanctuary, Archer allowed himself a low, satisfied chuckle. "Yes, yes," he said aloud, imagining his Janey present there with him and chiding him gently for his interference. "I know it's not the way you or Ilsa would handle such delicate matters, but it didn't turn out so badly, now, did it? I just gave her something to think about, tweaked the situation a little, that's all."

There was a soft rustling from the Norfolk pine, a sound as uncertain as an angel's exasperated sigh… probably nothing more than an insect alighting on a branch. But Archer returned to his gardening with a happy, hopeful heart.

KATIE STUFFED everything into the duffel bag, pulled out the new dresses, then jammed them back in again. She'd never had so much trouble packing before. That's what came of buying new clothes, of enjoying the feel of new fabric, of paying too much attention to what she wore. Adam had done that to her. Made her aware, self-conscious. Made her fall in love with him.

With a sigh, she sank to the floor and pulled everything out of the duffel. Time to start over. Begin anew. Quit while she was ahead. But her hand closed around the red dress and wouldn't let go. She'd been in love before…that heady, kick-up-your-heels state-of-being where colors were brighter and music was softer, and the whole world slowed to a waltz. It was one of her favorite experiences. But this wasn't like that. Since her conversation with Adam's grandfather earlier, this had become a roller coaster of a ride and she was scared, exhilarated, scared, off-balance...scared. Life was too short to feel like this. She'd wanted Adam's attention, sure. Had set out and schemed to get it. Maybe she'd even wanted him to fall in love with her. Well, of course, she had. What red-blooded American woman *wouldn't* want Adam Braddock besotted with love for her?

But Katie hadn't meant for it to be the real deal, the one true love of his life. Certainly not that. She'd thought—if she'd actually *thought* about it at all— that she and Adam might share a summer romance, something that ended when the party was over, not something that didn't...*gulp*...end at all.

Well, Mr. Braddock was wrong. That's all there was to it. She and Adam were barely even on the same planet. They had no future together. She'd dumped ice water on him and he was going to fire her. Period. End of story. She stuffed the red dress into the bag first this time, crushing it into the far corner, and tossing in everything else on top. She'd check in with the agency Monday, see what housing was available in Borneo. Or Alaska. That might be far enough away from here for her to find a nice forgetfulness.

Her hand closed over the plastic-covered sample pack of nail polish and she hesitated. Red, blue, lime green, purple, yellow, orange, pink, gold, silver and magenta. Circus colors. Ten of them. She did hate to miss the party. She'd worked really hard on it, and to quit now...well, it felt wrong, as if she'd been cheated. She'd never been in charge of planning anything before and, even though she'd had considerable help in decision-making from Ilsa, she'd made all the contacts, organized all the arrangements herself, actually *planned* the whole party. And she'd like to see it through. She'd told Mr. Braddock she would stay. Maybe she could, too. Really there was no reason she couldn't stay just one more week. Running away would work just as well a week from Sunday. It didn't have to happen today.

Except that Adam was going to fire her and it would be much harder to act like a party planner after that. Maybe she could appeal to his practical side, point out that he couldn't replace her at this late date—which Adam, being Adam, would take as a challenge to prove that he most certainly could replace her.

Katie sighed, resolutely set the nail polish in her give-away pile, and zipped the duffel bag. She was ready. One thing about traveling light, it didn't take long to pack. She glanced at her little travel clock. Six o'clock. Adam might even be home by now. She'd spent the day firming up details for the party. If she was going to get fired, she wanted Adam to know that she had, at least, done the job he'd begged her to do. He'd be sorry when he realized what a good job she'd done, too. He'd be sorry he hadn't listened to her. Sorry he hadn't trusted her. Sorry he hadn't been more careful about breaking her heart.

But that was the other thing about traveling light. No room for emotional baggage. Worst case scenario: she'd just have to leave her heart behind this time and let it catch up once it was on the mend. It was a shame really, that this experience couldn't have lasted a little longer. She liked it here, liked Braddock Hall, liked the town and the people in it.

Sitting back on her heels, she wondered what

would happen at the town council meeting on Saturday. Would the council vote to brick or not to brick? To put up flags or tinsel reindeer? She closed her eyes and imagined herself living here in Sea Change, owning a little tea and sandwich shop on Dockside Avenue, participating in the fusses that passed for city management in this quaint old town. Her fantasy grew by leaps and bounds—she decorated the tea and sandwich shop in eclectic motifs that could be changed on a whim; she campaigned for a seat on the council, won the election and voted Adam out of the chairmanship. Now that would be a fairy-tale ending, she decided.

A tap on her door popped the daydream in mideffervescent bubble.

"Mr. Adam would like to see you in his study," Abbott said when she opened the door.

Katie frowned. "When?"

The butler looked apologetic, as if he knew the axe was about to fall. "He's waiting for you now."

She got up. "I'll just put on my shoes."

"Miss Katie? I've, uh, taken the liberty of leaving a pitcher of water in Mr. Adam's study…in case you need it."

Her smile flashed in surprise. "Why, thank you, Abbott. I'm touched."

His lips barely made the bend to a smile, but his nod told her she wasn't without supporters in the household, even if their loyalty lay with Adam.

Of course, she'd have to be touched in the head to go near Adam with another water pitcher. She'd be lucky if he didn't empty one over her in retaliation. Still, it was a nice gesture for Abbott to have made. With a long, drawn-out sigh, she slipped on her sturdy Old Maine Trotters and headed downstairs to face the firing squad.

"COME IN, KATIE." Adam stood, tall and stern-looking behind his desk.

She lifted her chin from the safety of the doorway. "Abbott said you wanted to see me?"

"Close the door."

She stomped down the temptation to make a run for it while she still had the chance and reminded herself that she could have marched out while he was at the office, and she still had a full head of steam. He could have fussed and fumed to his heart's content once she was gone when it would have been no skin off her nose. But she hadn't done that. No, she'd waited around all day for him to come home and fire her because she'd told Mr. Braddock she would. And because Adam would have considered any other action cowardice. No way did she want him to think she was afraid to face him.

She wasn't, as it happened, so she closed the door and turned around, her knees shaking like yellow Jell-O, her backside as close to the door as she could get it. "Yes?" she said in her coolest tones. No way would she make this easy for him either.

"Did you catch the hem of your dress in the door?" he asked, pleasantly enough. "Looks like you may be trapped there."

She stepped into the center of the room to prove she was as loose as he was, and indifferent into the bargain. "Nope, not enough fabric in this dress for that." She gave an impulsive, self-conscious tug at the ruffled hem of the little black dress. "So if I had been caught between the door and the doorframe, you'd be facing a big fat personal injury lawsuit."

"I see." He moved slowly to the front of the desk. "Should I write you a check now?"

She blinked. "Wouldn't you rather wait until I'm actually injured?"

His lips curved in a slow smile and her stupid heart dropped like a rock at his feet. She *had* to get off of this roller coaster. "I was referring," he continued, "to the check for the five thousand I agreed to pay you for planning Grandfather's party."

"Oh." This certainly wasn't the way she thought these conversations usually began. "It was five thousand then and five thousand after the party," she reminded him because she wanted to sound professional. "Plus a very generous budget." She managed a Mona Lisa smile. "Oh, yes, and carte blanche. Don't forget that."

"No." He crossed his arms across his stomach. Not a particularly friendly gesture. "Nell tells me you never picked up your retainer. She says you never even called to ask about it."

Katie snapped her fingers. "I knew I forgot something."

He nodded, as if he believed her. "I intend to pay you for, uh, your services, Katie. I think you've earned it."

A ripple of anger flared from lukewarm to boiling, stiffening the backs of her knees. "If you're going to insult me, Adam, don't beat around the bush. I'd much rather you just came right out and accused me of being a prostitute, instead of just insinuating it!"

His arms dropped to his sides and his jaw went slack. "I beg your pardon?"

"You can beg it all you like, but believe me, there is no need for you to insult me just so you can feel justified in firing me. And just so you know, I was going to quit anyway." She spun for the door, furious, disbelieving...mortally wounded.

Amazingly, he beat her to the door and held it closed with one hand while reaching for her with the other. "Katie. Katie. Will you listen to me? I was not insulting you. I was trying to give you the five thousand dollars you've already earned in planning this party. It would *never* occur to me to...to try to pay you for what happened between us last night. That wouldn't be just an insult—to both of us, by the way—it would be an outright sacrilege."

She looked up, her fury deflating like a pricked balloon, quickly replaced by a heated embarrassment...and a sweet thrill at his last words. "A...a sacrilege?" she repeated, liking the sound of that.

"Or worse," he assured her. "You seem to jump to the wrong conclusions on the flimsiest of excuses."

"All this talk of money makes me nervous," she offered in a reedy voice. "I thought you called me down here to fire me."

"Fire you?" His grip on her arm changed from restraint to reassurance. "Why would you think that?"

She hated to bring this up. She really did. "Because of this morning. Because of the..." She made an eloquent gesture at the water pitcher, so thoughtfully provided by Abbott, the too-efficient butler. "You know."

His gaze followed the dispirited wave of her hand. "Ah, yes, the ice water. I imagine we ought to talk about that."

Her chin came up. "You deserved it."

"Hmm." He ran a hand the length of her lower arm, probably fully aware of how his touch affected her, of how it turned her resolve to mush. He was definitely taking unfair advantage. "I've been thinking about that most of the day. Thinking about you. And me."

"In between phone calls and faxes, you mean?"

"I didn't accomplish a blessed thing all day."

She peered up at him, hopeful. "Not even the first draft of an apology?"

He frowned at that. "I was sort of hoping we could call this morning's incident a draw."

"Not a chance. You behaved abominably."

"Oh, and dumping a gallon of ice water in my lap was right out of Miss Manner's rules of etiquette?"

She blushed, but wasn't backing down. With his hand on her arm, his fingertips stroking her as they were, she thought maybe she wasn't going to get fired after all. "Page 336," she said. "It's in the footnotes."

"You are a piece of work, Katie Canton," he said and kissed her.

Okay, so it wasn't the apology he owed her, but it would do in a pinch.

ADAM HADN'T MEANT to forgive her before getting the explanations he wanted, but he couldn't seem to stay focused when she was anywhere near him. Kissing, and other similar delights, were practically all he'd thought about the entire day. The minute she'd stepped inside his study, all flushed and saucy, well…it wasn't really so surprising that he'd forgotten the conversation he'd meant to have with her and seized temptation with greedy hands. For the moment, it was enough to know that last night hadn't been a trick of the moonlight or an accident of libido. Whatever magical spell she'd used on him before was still in force.

And then some.

When the kiss came to a sweetly reluctant end, he enclosed her in his arms and simply enjoyed the way her body fit against his, figuring as long as she was this close, she couldn't be reaching for idle water containers. But, with uncanny ability, she seemed to read his mind. "Just because you're an excellent kisser, Adam, doesn't mean I'm not still annoyed with you."

He tightened his hold on her, nuzzled her dark curls. "Sssh," he soothed. "Stay right where you are and see if the feeling passes."

"What if you just say you're sorry for the way you acted and I'll see how I feel about that?"

She felt really wonderful in his arms. "You have me at a disadvantage," he said.

"You bet I do. It's a God-given talent, too, so there's no point in fighting it. Just apologize and get it over with. Trust me, it's for the best."

"I meant, Katie, I'm not sure why you were upset with me this morning."

She stiffened. "Let me refresh your memory, then. *That was you?*" she mimicked. "The *waitress?*"

"You misunderstood," he said, happy to give his side. "I was surprised, yes, when—"

"Stunned," she corrected coolly.

"Stunned," he agreed. "When I realized we'd met before at The Torrid Tomato and that you were a waitress, not the party planner I assumed you to be when I talked to you on the phone. I was not casting aspersions on your field of endeavor or, for that matter, on the career of waiting tables, in general. I only thought you should have told me the truth the first time we talked."

She drew back a little, although he made no move to let her go, and she looked at him with skeptical astonishment. "You were appalled to discover I was a former waitress and Johnny-come-lately to this whole party-planning experience," she said. "Admit it."

He stiffened a little himself. "I believed you'd lied to me about who you were, yes."

Shaking her head, she looked at him with rueful sympathy. "Really, Adam, you desperately need to work on your listening skills." She patted the breast pocket of his suit coat. "I told you that first evening on the phone that you'd dialed the wrong number, had the wrong person. I said you'd made a mistake. I even told your secretary that when I talked to her, but you persisted, *insisted* I was who you'd decided I was, instead of just admitting you might have made a mistake."

He frowned, finding this a bit hard to swallow.

"Mrs. Fairchild told me at lunch that day she knew a reputable events planner and gave me the number."

"By mistake."

"She told you that?"

"No, but that's what it was. I gave her my number, wrote it on her business card because of the Tai Chi class. You probably weren't paying the slightest attention at the time. But afterward, somehow, she accidentally gave that card to you. But my point is that however the mix-up originally occurred, this whole misunderstanding could have been prevented if you'd actually listened to what I said instead of proceeding on what you'd already decided was true."

He narrowed his gaze on her. "And you're completely innocent in this lack of meaningful communication? It was all entirely my fault?"

She had the grace to look a trifle guilty. "Well, Adam, you are a very persuasive man, and you did offer me a ride in a Rolls-Royce. And consider this, if I hadn't given up on trying to convince you not to hire me, you wouldn't be here now, about to spend quite another spectacular night." She smiled up at him and that was all it took. He kissed her again.

Halfway through her very satisfying response, his private phone rang. And, by reflex, he answered.

JUST WHEN Katie had begun to think maybe her heart and Adam's might have a great deal in common after all, he answered his phone. His conversation took him away from her in a heartbeat, and she resented the interruption almost as much as she begrudged the caller his focused and intense attention. What had she been thinking…even for a moment? He would never give up this life, never sacrifice the adrenaline rush of a business deal for the relaxed, live-in-the-moment life she treasured. And she could never fit into his world. She liked going barefoot and traveling light much too much to be content within the structure of the rules he lived by every moment of every day. His middle name was responsibility. Hers, varied from day to day. Even if he could change, even if she could bear to ask him to, it would never work.

Once the newness of his experience with her wore off, he'd probably answer his phone in the middle of making love to her. And he would never understand why she might resent that. He was all business, all the time already, and any moments she managed to steal from Braddock Industries would be costly. With a sigh, she slipped free of his embrace.

He didn't even seem to notice. ''Of course. I'll meet you at the hangar in—'' he glanced at his ever-present watch ''—an hour. Yes, Lara, I know. I'm leaving right now.''

Cutting off the call, he offered Katie an apologetic smile and tipped up her chin with his fingers. ''I have to leave,'' he said. ''An emergency. I'll have Nell get that check to you and if you haven't already, be sure your resource people know to send their bills to my office.''

''Anything else?'' she asked, wishing he were a different kind of man, more like her, less focused, often impulsive, and that he didn't always have on shoes with a high-gloss finish. ''Any other instructions I should follow?''

He smiled, not even aware her sadness went deeper than this simple goodbye. ''Yes,'' he said.

''Wait for me.'' He leaned in, kissed her sweetly, and left her there.

It was, Katie thought, only marginally better than being fired.

Chapter Ten

Ilsa arrived and the tensions at Braddock Hall shifted. Like a broken clock that suddenly starts counting down the minutes in double time, the upcoming party took on a life of its own and although Katie was busier than she'd thought possible, she couldn't help but notice the change in the Braddock men. Adam remained away on his emergency, didn't even call in from the West Coast, where Nell reported he was. That, in itself, reinforced Katie's opinion of where she ranked in his priorities. He had time to keep in touch with his office, but not a moment to spare for her.

But she tried not to think about that, concentrating instead on dealing with the million little problems that arose around the party plans. That, and watching Bryce and Peter regard Ilsa with suspicious eyes, while Archer went out of his way to be charming to her and James vacillated between jumping to attention every time she walked into a room and pretending not to notice her presence. Night Owl Monica turned into a hawk, shadowing her fiancé's every move with an eagle eye and boring anyone who would listen with her involved accounts of shopping expeditions, past and future. Ilsa, cool, calm and collected, gave no inkling that she wasn't having a perfectly marvelous time.

Katie found it all very interesting, but her attempts to get Ilsa's feelings on the stir her presence had caused among the Braddock men met with a polite, but diplomatic, "Really? I hadn't noticed."

By the time Saturday arrived, Katie was thoroughly disgusted with the diplomacy that seemed to stalk the Hall like some gentleman ghost, echoing varying versions of *"Pardon me. Excuse me, please. Pardon. Oops, no offense meant. Pardon. Soooo sorry."* Bryce and Peter were obviously fearful Ilsa would somehow usurp their grandmother's vacant place in the household and didn't want to show either animosity or encouragement. So they played a polite game of diplomatic tag. *"Good evening, Mrs. Fairchild, how are you this evening? Lovely outfit. You must be missing being in your own home. Planning any trips abroad in the near future? Greece is a great spot to spend the winter, you know."* James was even worse with his conscientious and singular efforts to renew his acquaintance with Ilsa without annoying either Monica or his father. Monica kept James on a short leash, and Archer watched the whole charade with a dignified glee, being just attentive enough to his special guest to keep everyone guessing.

No one, with the possible exception of Monica, who never said anything of interest, anyway, seemed capable of speaking their minds. Except, of course, for the caterers and tent rental folks, who couldn't or wouldn't do all they'd guaranteed they would without a great deal of diplomacy from Katie, who found she had little aptitude for it, and even less patience. Who knew a party could be so much work?

It didn't help that there was still no sign of Adam or that no one else seemed to miss him, at all. For all Katie knew, he'd eloped with the mysterious Lara and was honeymooning at his office in the Bahamas. If, of course, Braddock Industries *had* an office in the Bahamas. She pretended she didn't mind his silence, and she followed his instructions to the letter, accepting the check Nell sent and tucking it inside the duffel she didn't unpack, telling the caterer and all the rest to submit their final invoices to Nell for payment.

And she waited, telling herself this was a positive experience, too. Listening to cars driving up, footsteps, the far-off sound of a familiar voice coming closer, closer...the hope that fluttered like a caged bird each and every time. *Was it him? Was he here? In a moment, would she see him, touch him, welcome him home?* The anticipation was exquisite and terrible, and made her so anxious, she knew with a heart-deep resignation that she must be in love.

At night, she lay in bed and tried to feel the width and breadth and depth of the emotion, told herself that to explore it, welcome it, wallow in it would be the first step in getting over it. But each night, as the wonderful old house fell asleep around her, she lay in bed, still wide awake, wondering why after all this time, after all her efforts to stay on the move, following one adventure into another, her heart had stubbornly settled on this place as home, this family as the one where she belonged—and Adam, as the stone wall she couldn't get over.

ADAM ARRIVED home to find the birthday party in full swing. After a week of chasing Lara's worthless brother up and down the West Coast from Seattle to Tijuana, he was exhausted and thought at first he was hallucinating. But after a few deliberate blinks and squints, he realized there really were ponies on the lawn and costumed clowns all over the place, and, apparently, a full-blown circus at Braddock Hall. There were guests, around two hundred of them, some in evening dress, some in costume, and there were jugglers, acrobats, and an Uncle Sam on stilts. What in hell was going on? If there was an elephant on the veranda, he was going to have a holy fit.

Without even going inside to change clothes, as he'd intended, Adam made his way through the scattered crowd—most of whom did seem to be having a rollicking good time—around to the huge red-striped tent that occupied a good portion of the south grounds. It was a circus. A real one, although he hadn't as yet spied the elephant. There was popcorn and snow cones and peanuts being served by waitstaff in clown suits, their faces painted in gaudy smiles. "Good evening, Mr. Adam," one of them— Good Lord, was that Abbott?—said as he passed. "Welcome home."

Welcome home. Bah humbug.

Katie saw him first and her smile almost—*almost*—made up for the fiasco of an evening she'd planned to celebrate his grandfather's birthday. He'd thought about her constantly while he was away, wanted, no, *ached,* to be with her again. Was this her idea of a joke? Of thumbing her nose at the traditions of his proud and noble family? But why? And why hadn't he kept better tabs on what she was doing? Why had he so carelessly given her carte blanche? Why hadn't he had even an inkling she was planning something like this?

Because she hadn't asked for money. If she'd approached Nell even once, the fat would have been in the fire. Nell would have questioned a requisition for an elephant and he would have stopped this disaster before it got started. Katie, the woman he had missed so badly for the major part of every day for more than a week, the woman he was beginning to believe he loved, had been planning all that time to make a fool of him and his whole family. By the time she reached him in the crowd, he was furious beyond reason. "What is the meaning of this?" he asked before she'd even reached him, hating the fact that his heart beat faster with every step that brought her nearer.

"Isn't it great? Your grandfather is having the best time. He's…" She looked over her shoulder, straining to see Archer in the crowd. "Well, he was on the tightrope walk a minute ago."

"The tightrope?" Adam hoped she had enough sense to have an ambulance standing by. "You let my seventy-nine-year-old grandfather walk the tightrope?"

She looked at him then, her brows below her silk top hat drawing together in a questioning frown. "It's not *high*. He's not going to get hurt on it, if that's what you're worried about."

"I'm *worried* about you, Katie, and what maggot of insanity caused you to put together something like *this*." His hand swept out to encompass the whole party with his displeasure. "Why would you think, for one second, that I hired you to plan a parody of a party for my grandfather's birthday?"

The question cleared on her face, her own displeasure coming to the forefront. *"This—"* she aped his gesture with an exaggerated wave of her hand. "—happens to be the kind of party he wanted. You know how I know that, Adam? I *asked* him and then, I *listened* to what he said. What a concept, huh? Maybe you should try it sometime." Whirling around, she bumped into a clown wearing a car. It was a cardboard car, suspended around his hefty middle by straps that ran front to back across his wide shoulders. "Great party," the clown—Holden Locke, as it turned out on slightly closer glance—said to Adam. "Most fun I've had while fully clothed since Bryce and I won the Block Island Regatta. Are you going to share the name of your events person, or am I going to have to find that out for myself?"

"He called 1-800-WAITRESS and got lucky," Katie said, her voice tight with anger. "Neat trick, huh?" She was gone in a swath of vivid color and Adam, belatedly, noticed she was wearing the red coat and black hat of a ringmaster. No shoes, of course, but colorful ruffs of fabric circled her bare ankles and, unless he was mistaken, each of her ten toenails had been painted a different garish color.

"Wow," Holden said, his tone low and appreciative, his gaze appraising the long, bare length of her shapely legs. "She can tame my lion any day."

Adam's fist clenched with a sudden intense desire to punch the clown in the car suit, but Holden turned away, beeping a lusty *ah-oog-ga* on his car horn as he followed the curves of a woman in a gold leotard. The Girl on the Flying Trapeze, no doubt. "Hey, Adam." It was Peter, wearing a tux, which for some reason made the scene around them seem even more surreal. "When did you get home?"

"Have you been gone?" Bryce asked, moving up next to Peter, his yellow plaid shirt coupled with Adam's red tie making a strange compromise between the circus world and an ordinary, and normally very conservative, Braddock party.

"I just got in," Adam said shortly, his gaze seeking through the crowd for another glimpse of Katie.

"Well, you're not dressed for the party, that's for sure," Peter observed. "Katie got a costume for you, too. I put it in your room this afternoon myself."

Adam would have been happier not knowing that. "I'm not dressing up like Bozo for anyone."

"That *would* be redundant in your case," Bryce said, a teasing glint in his eye. "Where have you been this week, if it's not some big industry secret?"

"California," Adam answered. "Helping Lara locate her nephew."

"Where is she now?" Peter looked past Adam, as if he expected Lara to be there.

"Please tell me you moved her lock, stock and portfolio to the West Coast," Bryce suggested. "California deserves her."

Adam frowned at his middle brother. "She's recovering from a nasty confrontation with her witless brother. He decided, after four years of ignoring the fact that he's a father, he should spend some time with his son. Unfortunately, the courts tend to look on that as kidnapping.''

''Wow,'' Peter said. ''He stole the kid?''

''It's a mess, legally and emotionally, although Calvin—that's the little boy—seemed to take it all in stride.''

''Jeez,'' Peter said, his sympathies instantly with the child. ''Lara doesn't deserve the family she got stuck with.''

''Does anyone?'' But the fun had gone out of Bryce and he looked troubled, even concerned. ''So is Lara okay?''

Adam caught a flash of red and black over by the snow cone bar. ''Sure,'' he said. ''Lara can handle anything. Excuse me.'' And he started through the crowd, hoping to catch up to her and get some further explanation for this travesty of a party.

But he was waylaid by his father halfway there and when he craned his neck to see around Uncle Sam's wooden leg, the ringmaster had disappeared. ''Adam,'' James said in a voice lowered, so as not to be overheard. ''Where have you been all week? Ilsa's moved into the Hall and I'm very much afraid that your grandfather is *involved* with her.''

Adam had figured out a few things about his grandfather's *special* friend since reading the dossier Lara had put together for him before her family crisis occurred, but he didn't think it was his place to share the information. ''There's no reason to worry, Dad, believe me. She and Grandfather are just friends.''

James did not look convinced. ''I don't know,

Adam. They slip off together, down to the solarium. I've seen them. No telling what they do there.''

A smile tapped Adam, but only briefly. ''They probably talk about gardening. I think her thumb is nearly as green as his.''

''They seem awfully secretive about it.''

Adam clapped a hand on his father's tuxedo-clad shoulder—Monica probably wouldn't allow him to wear a costume—and tried for a reassuring tone. ''It's nothing. They've just discovered a mutual interest, made a...connection that's all.''

''There you are, darling.'' Monica, in classic black, came out of the colorful crowd to claim her man.

''Adam, welcome home.'' It was Ilsa Fairchild, looking gorgeous and glamorous in the glittery robes and headdress of a circus performer. Next to her, Monica's black couture lost all its class, and her beauty looked merely youthful and untested. ''Hello again, James. Monica.'' Ilsa's confident smile encompassed them all before she slipped her hand through Adam's arm and led him away, leaving James looking longingly after them. ''What do you think of the party?'' she asked when they'd taken a few steps. ''Isn't she an original?''

''I think that's safe to say,'' Adam agreed, committed to *not* discussing Katie with Mrs. Fairchild. ''I'm sorry I haven't been here this week for your visit. I hope you've enjoyed your stay.''

She considered him and the slightly cool note in his voice with a curious gaze. ''Yes,'' she said. ''I have, thanks.''

"Any…connections…come up this week I should know about?"

Her curiosity melted into understanding. "Ah, you've found me out, I see. Did Archer let it slip?"

"No. I did a bit of investigating," he said, liking her all the more for not pretending. "Discovered exactly what type of public relations IF Enterprises provides."

Her smile was easy and warm. "Then you probably are aware of my company's success rate." It was part statement, part question and Adam debated whether to answer.

But why equivocate now? She was a matchmaker of quite extraordinary talents and probably knew better than he did that she had put together yet another successful connection. "I would never want to argue with your record," he said, letting the decision come to him just like that. "But I would like to know how you came to choose such an unlikely match this time."

"All I did was introduce the possibilities, Adam. You made the choice all on your own."

"With a little help from Katie." A smile found him and he couldn't have made it go away if he tried.

"I love it when a plan comes together," Ilsa said, giving his arm a conspiratorial squeeze. "I do hope you won't blow my cover with your brothers. It could make the next connection—" she made a face "—difficult."

"It'll be our secret," Adam assured her. "I won't even tell Dad."

She looked startled, but recovered nicely. "Oh,

well, I'm sure he wouldn't care one way or the other, but maybe it's best if—''

"There you are!" Archer approached, his cane tapping in his hurry. "What in hell did you say to Katie?" he asked Adam without preamble. "She was crying, blubbering out some bizarre apology to me, as if I hadn't been telling her for weeks I wanted a *real* birthday party and not some squeaky-clean, boring affair with an obligatory cake and a million candles."

A wave of regret washed over Adam. He'd done it again. Hurt Katie by not giving her a chance to explain, by not listening when she'd tried to tell him the truth. "Where is she? I've got to talk to her."

Abbott, looking strangely out of character in his costume, appeared like magic. "Miss Katie has left, sir. Just now. I tried to get her to let Benson drive her, but she took Ruth's bicycle instead and rode off with her duffel bag."

Archer's frown swung straight to Adam. "I can't believe I raised such an idiot." He used his cane to tap Adam's leg, suggesting action was urgently required. "Well, don't just stand there. Go after her."

"Who?" Bryce ambled up in time to hear the last. "Is Lara in trouble again already?"

"No," Adam said, turning to go. "I am."

"You?" Bryce's disbelieving laugh followed Adam as he headed for the house, Abbott at his heels.

"I took the liberty of asking Benson to bring the Rolls around, sir," the butler said when they reached the foyer. "He should be waiting for you outside." In two long strides, Abbott moved ahead of Adam to open the door. "She's headed in the direction of Sea Change."

"Thank you, Abbott."

"Bring her back, sir."

Adam didn't reply as he ran down the steps to the Rolls. Ignoring Benson and the open back door, he got behind the wheel and reached for the key. "Benson!" he yelled, frustrated and in a frenzy to find Katie. "I'll drive myself."

A moment later, the key was in his hand and the chauffeur was stepping away from the car, calling a muffled, "Good luck, sir," as the luxury engine purred to life and Adam headed for town.

The bicycle caught the headlights, its reflectors glinting in the dark. It was leaning against the empty store front that once had been Willford's Antiques and Treasures. Duncan Willford had come to Sea Change from Albuquerque and lasted two years before he closed up shop and returned to the West. He hadn't been well-liked in Sea Change. Outsiders never were. But there, in front of his failed venture, stood a ringmaster, a woman who had come to Sea Change for adventure and turned Adam's plans on their ear. He hadn't known it was possible to love anyone, anything so much until the moment he saw her standing there in the beam of the headlights, looking like she'd lost her best friend.

"Hi," he said, getting out of the car.

"I've got pepper spray," she said, challenging him even in her obvious misery. "And I know how to use it, too."

"I don't doubt it for a second." He moved closer, forming an apology as he edged around the front of the Rolls. "I'll be careful not to make any sudden moves."

"See that you don't. I'm not in a very good mood and my finger might just accidentally slip."

"I'm sure whatever happens, I will have deserved it."

She perked up a little at that, squinted at him in the gold glow of the streetlights. "What are you doing here?" she asked. "Because if you came to get your money back, you can forget it. I don't care what you think of the party, I earned every penny and I'm not giving it back."

"I came to get you, Katie."

"Well, I'm not going back either. I told your grandfather goodbye and you can tell the others whatever you want. I'm not making any apologies."

"Not even for your very unprofessional behavior?" He took another step, keeping an eye on her trigger finger...although it looked as if she were empty-handed.

"If you'd ever listened to me, you'd know I wasn't a professional to begin with."

"I need to learn how to listen better," he agreed. "It might save us from having to have these kinds of confrontations in the future."

She cocked her head. "I can't see that as a big problem since we aren't likely to be within a hundred miles of each other in the future."

"It's going to be hard to have a relationship at that distance."

"Relationship?"

He shrugged. "I'm not saying it couldn't be done,

just that I think it would be much more enjoyable at closer range.''

''What are you talking about, Adam?''

''Love, marriage, happily ever after.''

In the ensuing quiet, he could hear the hum of electricity in the old-fashioned pole lights and the heavy *thud-thud-thud* of his heartbeat. ''Have you been drinking?'' she asked finally. ''Because it sounds like you've had one too many snow cones tonight.''

''I only returned from helping my friend resolve a sticky family crisis in time to make a complete fool of myself at my grandfather's birthday party. There hasn't been time for snow cones or even to change into my clown costume.'' He took his heart in his hands and reached for her. ''I'm so sorry, Katie. I was exhausted from the trip and so eager to see you and, well, I wasn't expecting to find a three-ring circus going on in my backyard.''

''If you'd asked, I would have told you exactly what I had planned.''

He hated that he'd caused that wounded note in her voice, hated that he'd caused her any pain at all. ''I'm willing to sit still while you dump a whole tub of ice water in my lap if it will help make amends.''

''Oh, it would take more ice than I could find in Rhode Island to do that,'' she said, sounding slightly more sassy. ''But you know what? I'll just forgive you and you can go on back home with a clear conscience. Consider it my gift to you on the occasion of your grandfather's seventy-ninth birthday.''

''I love you, Katie,'' he said simply.

She didn't seem surprised. "Despite my unprofessional behavior? That's a bit difficult to believe."

"I think I told you very recently that it would be most unprofessional of you to break my heart, but you seem quite eager to do it, anyway."

That stopped her. "I didn't, couldn't break your heart, Adam. You've got it very carefully wrapped around Braddock Industries. Mine, I'm afraid, wasn't so well protected."

Hope surged through him with unrestrained eagerness. "Give me a chance, Katie. Marry me. Take me on your next adventure and the next one after that. Save me from myself."

She closed the distance between them, placed her hand lovingly on his chest. "That's not fair, Adam, and it's too much responsibility for anyone to take on. You have to make your own choices, make the life you want. And admit it, you love being Adam Braddock, CEO. It's who you are."

"No, it's who I became because I thought it was my birthright, the duty I inherited because I was born and abandoned by my parents. I thought I owed it to my grandparents to become the man my father wasn't. I thought it was my responsibility to take care of my brothers, because they were abandoned, too. I want to be different, Katie. I want to be the man I am when I'm with you—happy, not always knowing what's next, but putting up my chin and heading bravely into the unknown. You've given me a glimpse of the free spirit I've kept caged inside me, given me a taste of the adventure real love can be. It's too late to run away from that, now."

"I'm not running away," she said, too quickly.

"Aren't you, Katie? Aren't you running from the possibility that you've stumbled into a place that feels like home, into the arms of a man who needs you and whom, I believe, you need, too." He stopped, decided honesty was the best policy. "In my briefcase at the Hall, I have a report on you, Katie. A background check. A list of all your jobs, where you've lived, what schools you attended. There's an accounting of the fire that started when your father fell asleep with a cigarette in his hands and robbed you of your mother and your baby sister. It states that your father committed suicide and that you were raised by your paternal grandparents. What it doesn't say is how brave you were to go on living. It can't reveal the courage you've shown in becoming not a bitter and vengeful person, but one who brings joy and laughter into every moment that you're alive. I don't know how you came to be so free, Katie, but wherever you go and whatever you do, I want to be there with you. To protect you, if it's ever necessary, but mainly to learn a little of how you do it and maybe to give you back just a little of the love you've denied yourself for so long." He reached out and wiped away the solitary teardrop that glistened on her cheek. "I've been waiting all my life to love you, Katie. If it takes the rest of my life, I'll prove that to you."

She nestled into his arms like a runaway child who finally has come home. "This won't be easy," she said at last, her voice shaken, but steady.

"Maybe," he said, tipping her face up to his. "But I'm a very fast learner."

"It'll mean no cell phones, no faxes—no shoes."

His smile was slow, but infinitely grateful. "I'll adjust. On the other hand, you may someday get tired of traveling light and want to invest in a bigger suitcase, maybe a diaper bag or two."

Uncertainty lined her Mona Lisa smile. "That sounds suspiciously like a real proposal. You should probably quit while you're ahead."

So he kissed her, thinking ahead to the experiences they'd collect together, the life they'd build one precious moment at a time. Someday he'd tell her that they'd had a little help from a matchmaker of distinction, but not now.

Now, was this single moment, when holding Katie and loving Katie was the only thing that mattered. Come to think of it, he couldn't imagine anything would ever be more important than that.

* * * * *

The BILLION DOLLAR BRADDOCKS

series will continue.
Watch for Bryce's story,
coming in March from
Harlequin American Romance.

This Mother's Day Give Your Mom A Royal Treat

Win a fabulous one-week vacation in Puerto Rico for you and your mother at the luxurious Inter-Continental San Juan Resort & Casino. The prize includes round trip airfare for two, breakfast daily and a mother and daughter day of beauty at the beachfront hotel's spa.

INTER·CONTINENTAL
San Juan
RESORT & CASINO

Here's all you have to do:

Tell us in 100 words or less how your mother helped with the romance in your life. It may be a story about your engagement, wedding or those boyfriends when you were a teenager or any other romantic advice from your mother. The entry will be judged based on its originality, emotionally compelling nature and sincerity. See official rules on following page.

Send your entry to:
Mother's Day Contest

In Canada	**In U.S.A.**
P.O. Box 637	P.O. Box 9076
Fort Erie, Ontario	3010 Walden Ave.
L2A 5X3	Buffalo, NY
	14269-9076

Or enter online at www.eHarlequin.com

PRROY